NILE SPARROWS

NILE SPARROWS

Ibrahim Aslan

Translated by
Mona El-Ghobashy

The American University in Cairo Press
Cairo   New York

Dar el Kutub No. 16137/03
ISBN 977 424 828 7

Designed by Sarah Rifky/AUC Press Design Center
Printed in Egypt

For Hisham and Shadi

Translator's Note

"I KNEW THE novel form was important," says Ibrahim Aslan, "but I didn't know why." He put aside early drafts for *Nile Sparrows* and began working on a renewed examination of the novel, what would become his novella *Wardiyat layl* ('Night Shift,' 1992). It then took him five years to complete *Nile Sparrows*, which shares the Nile-side setting and some peripheral characters with his debut novel *Malik al-hazin* ('The Heron,' 1983). For Aslan, the writer of atmospheric short stories, describing moods and emotions in a novel is a qualitatively different, and more difficult, task.

In this translation I have tried to convey the subtle and evocative moods conjured by the author. I have retained the spare prose and elliptical, dialogue-driven narrative that invites the reader to let the imagination wander in the eloquent silences and nuances of what is left unsaid. The frequent narrative movement back and forward through time is anchored by the setting of Fadlallah Uthman Street, the modest road where the main characters live, in Aslan's own neighborhood of Warraq, near Imbaba. The street is also a metaphorical anchor, standing silent witness to the passage of time and the aging and death of its kindhearted, sociable denizens.

While there is one omniscient though unobtrusive narrative voice, it shifts with the alternating focus on different characters, bending to take on their dispositions and internal states of mind. Like a Nile sparrow, the authorial 'eye' flits from one character to another, resting just long enough to give us either a full-blown portrait or an eloquent snapshot before moving on to another person and another story in another time.

Aslan told me this novel "has an Egyptian spirit," and indeed, while invoking universal human themes and relations, it does so in a distinctly Egyptian idiom. Egyptian staples such as *fuul* (fava beans), *karkadeh* (hibiscus tea), and *mulukhiya* (Jew's mallow) figure prominently. Egyptian family customs are especially important, such as the practice of naming young children after older family members while the latter are still alive, as the young Hanem is named after her sprightly grandmother and the young Abdalla after his pensive older cousin. The Arab practice of calling parents "Abu" ('father of') and "Umm" ('mother of') is also ubiquitous, as Nargis and al-Bahey Uthman are Umm Abdalla and Abu Abdalla (or Abduh, a diminutive of Abdalla).

Understanding Egyptian marriage customs is important to make sense of Abd al-Reheem's four consecutive unions. The first phase is the engagement, then the signing of the marriage contract, and finally the public wedding ceremony and moving into the new home. The signing of the contract and the wedding are usually done together, but often there is an interval between the engagement and the marriage while the couple get to know each other better and save up for the accoutrements of their new home. To assure their commitment and allow them to meet alone and move about freely in public without social censure, the couple signs the marriage contract and are legally married, but the union is not fully consummated until the wedding ceremony. The practice of dating is unknown, and particularly in traditional families in the first half of the twentieth century such as Afkar and Abd al-Reheem's, the signing of the contract was especially important to protect the woman's reputation and to assure the commitment of her partner. Often, disagreements develop between a legally married couple and they divorce before consummating their union, as happens with Afkar and Abd al-Reheem. Marriages are also common between couples who, for one reason or another, wish to keep their unions unknown to relatives, employers, or the state, such as Abd al-Reheem's short-lived marriage to Inshiraah. Legally, these unions are no different from publicly announced marriages; they also require the presence of two witnesses, and as with any marriage contract, can be annulled by divorce.

I thank Ibrahim Aslan for writing this novel and for our enjoyable conversations about it. I also thank Mandy McClure for her excellent suggestions for a more flowing translation, and Sayed El-Ghobashy, who adopted the craft of translation and brought to it the rigor and precision that is his wont. I dedicate to him this translation as a belated retirement gift.

1

THE GRANDMOTHER AWOKE from her nap. She left her place by
the large, clay water-storage urn and walked to the door barefoot, holding onto the wall for support. She stood concealing
her body in the doorjamb, looking out at her son, Abd al-
Reheem, who was being carried to the open car. She kept smiling and talking to herself until the crowd dispersed. Hagg
Mahmoud the coal dealer spotted her and went over.

"You go inside, Auntie Hanem. God willing, he'll be fine."

"Who are you, son?"

"I'm Hagg Mahmoud."

"Oh my, Dawlat's son?"

"No, I'm Hagg Mahmoud, the coal dealer."

"The coal man?"

"Yes."

"And when did you come, son?"

"I've been here for a while."

"Welcome, please come in."

"Thank you," he said.

"No, that won't do...."

"It's all right. You go in because of the crowds."

"God protect you from harm. Where are they carrying that
boy, Abd al-Reheem?"

"I'll go see and come back to tell you."

The grandmother said, "Not again, Abd al-Reheem. It must be election time again." Then she asked Mahmoud, "You want to go to them, son?"

"Yes, I'll change clothes and catch up with them."

"You'll find them by the shops, at the beginning of town. You see, Manshawi Pasha won."

Mahmoud turned his head and said, "Almighty God, the poor woman."

"You honor us by your presence, son. Welcome, welcome."

She turned her small frame and let out a chuckle, "Dalal, girl! Hee, hee, hee!" and she went inside.

Amina was in the kitchen, and Mr. Abdalla ibn Uthman was sitting in the living room, sipping coffee and smoking, watching television and spotting his older son through the half open door of the bedroom as he tried on all his clothes in front of the mirror. The young one, who was lying on the big chair, his head on one armrest and his legs hanging over the other, was watching the television screen and trying to resist sleep. The young host was standing in the middle of a group of young students at the foot of the pyramids, asking them how many there were and the names of who built them. The students would raise their hands and answer, "Khufu, Khafre, Menkaure," while their teacher would sometimes appear on screen and then disappear:

"Okay, who knows why the ancient Egyptians built the pyramids?" asked the host.

Nobody answered at first, then one boy raised his hand.

"Go ahead, dear," she said as she placed the microphone near his face.

"They built the pyramids so they could bury Mr. Principal there," the boy said.

"Oh my goodness!" the host and the dozing boy laughed, and Mr. Abdalla also laughed and put out his cigarette. He thought of getting up to tell Amina what the boy said, but the canary call of the doorbell filled the living room.

It was Salama, Mr. Abdalla's middle brother. And because he came unannounced, Mr. Abdalla waited to hear what was wrong. His worries were confirmed when he saw Salama sitting with his legs apart, his elbow resting on his knee, looking at him silently. He didn't want to ask questions, preferring to smile and delay speaking, taking care that the delay not extend for too long so he could appear normal, to force Salama to talk without asking. This was all because Mr. Abdalla did not like the seriousness contrived by his brother every time he came to him with his latest news, bad most of the time and having to do with the family. It bothered him more that Salama would conceal what looked like a smile while staring at him, or peer at the refrigerator in the corner, as he was doing now, as if he hadn't seen this refrigerator dozens of times before, as if he wanted to scare him, or at least worry him, when he of all people should know that his older brother had already received the worst news and that it was no longer easy to scare him. That's why Mr. Abdalla was not pleased. The silence between them was about to turn ridiculous were it not for Amina appearing out of the kitchen to say, "How are you, Abu Amal, and how's Samia?"

Salama straightened up and said with real anguish, "We haven't slept for two days, Umm Esam."

"Is one of the kids sick or what?"

"I wish." He took out his pack of cigarettes and busied himself with it.

3

Since the topic was finally broached, Mr. Abdalla asked quietly, "What's going on?"

"It's Grandma Hanem."

"What, she died too?"

"I wish."

"What do you mean, you wish?"

"Because when someone dies we know where they are, but she's just disappeared."

"How did she disappear?"

"Like a grain of salt in water."

"Grandma Hanem?"

Salama nodded.

"When did this happen?"

"Dalal says a few days ago."

He blew out some cigarette smoke and said that for their part, there was no place where they hadn't looked, every house on Fadlallah Uthman, the streets around Fadlallah Uthman, police stations, hospitals, even the morgue. "We searched there too," said Salama.

"Oh, my God," said Amina.

"Hagg Mahmoud the coal dealer was just at the morgue two hours ago," Salama said.

Mr. Abdalla was very bewildered. "Where could she have gone?"

"I think maybe, God only knows, she went to the village."

"What village? And to see whom? It's been thirty years since she's been there."

He thought for a while and added, "And how would she get there? She's over ninety."

Salama said, "Grandma is 140 years old today."

"So what are you saying?"

"I'm saying you have to travel."

"Travel where?"

"To the village." Salama's tone of voice changed, and he explained that if their grandmother was in the village now and nobody asked after her, they would say that her daughter's children let her travel alone at her age. "And that would be a scandal," he said. And besides, Abdalla was the only one among them who knew the village as a young man. "So you're the one who's got to go now, right?" he said.

"Right," said Amina.

Mr. Abdalla said, "You want me to go there and talk to who?"

"To whoever. At least we'd have asked after her," said Salama, spreading his arms over the armrests. "Where's the tea, Umm Esam?"

"It's almost ready, Abu Amal."

Mr. Abdalla finished shaving his white-flecked stubble. He put on one of his ironed shirts and polished the shoes he rarely used. He stood before the mirror arranging his hair, which had gone almost completely white.

On the way to his uncle's house, his feelings—which rarely betrayed him—told him that he'd see his uncle's wife, Dalal, standing in the doorway with her smiling face, telling him that they found her, and he'd step into his grandmother's small darkened room at the end of the long hallway. He'd see her on the rug in her black dress, and they would laugh together as he told her how Salama thought she was lost. Then he would sit with Dalal in the large room, have tea, and return home.

So Mr. Abdalla started off, entering Fadlallah Uthman Street from the end that opened onto the big empty suq grounds north of the Nile. Every time he came to Fadlallah Uthman he felt embarrassed about his age. He was thinking about this as he passed Muhammad Effendi al-Rashidi's old dusty car underneath the closed window of their old apartment. Fadlallah Uthman was about to come to an end now, at Qatr al-Nada, which extended east to the Nile and west to the city, where his uncle's house was. From where he stood, he could see the distant entrance to the house, and when he got closer he realized that it was open.

Dalal was sitting on the plastic mat spread out near the open entrance. As soon as she saw him, she burst out crying. Mr. Abdalla made his way to the large room now feeling truly burdened, and he sat wanting to know everything in detail. The room accommodated a wide bed, an Asyuti living room set, and an old-fashioned couch under the long window. And on the faded green wall was a black-and-white photograph in an old, gold frame. But Dalal did not have much to add to what Salama had already said. She noticed on Saturday that she heard no movement in the house, and when she went to Grandma Hanem's room she wasn't there, and when she found that the slippers had disappeared, she was sure that she'd gone out.

"What slippers? Was she used to going out?" asked Mr. Abdalla.

"Never."

"So what do you mean?"

Dalal explained that from the day her daughter Nargis had died, Grandmother Hanem had been looking for her slippers so she could put them on and go to her. And when she finally began to forget about this, her son Abd al-Reheem died, and she again started looking for the slippers to put them on and go see her children, and that's why Dalal hid them from her behind the large, clay water-storage urn.

"Where'd she want to go see them?"

"God only knows."

"Maybe she went to the cemetery?"

"No, she thinks they're still alive."

"Alive?"

"Of course." Dalal turned to her son Abdalla who was sitting cross-legged on a corner of the bed. "Boy, get up and get a box of tea."

Mr. Abdalla looked at his namesake, whom he usually ignored, lit a cigarette and said, "Where do you think she could've gone?"

"The only place is the village."

"Could she get there alone?"

"Maybe she asked someone and they led her there."

Mr. Abdalla said, "Very strange."

"You have to go tomorrow, Mr. Abdalla."

"God willing."

"Please, Abu Esam." With that, she got up to make tea. He stood up and approached the old, gold frame, studying the picture at the front of which sat his mother Nargis, still in full health, and next to her Grandma Hanem, tiny in her black veil. Behind them was his uncle, Abd al-Reheem, a portly young man with long parted hair. While he was standing, the power went out and Dalal came in carrying the big, black kerosene lamp. She put it on the long windowsill, the window's upper half open onto dark Fadlallah Uthman.

2

ONCE, THE POWER had gone out suddenly while Nargis was watching television. She was terrified because there was nothing she feared more in the whole world than the dark. She took one step while waiting for Bahey, who was at Gaber the grocer's. When she heard the brush of his gallabiya against the door, she called out, "Abu Abduh?"

"Yes," said Bahey and went into the kitchen.

Nargis stood listening to his hands fiddle with the matchbox and saw the faint light as he was coming through the hallway. She watched as the shadow made by the towel hanging on the nail got bigger on the floor mat, then moved to the wall and shrank in the light of the kerosene lamp that he held between his hands.

Bahey saw Nargis in this state and smiled. He put the lamp on the television and wiped its warm glass with his palms, then raised it, asking Nargis about the matchbox he asked her to keep and use if the power went out. She returned to her place on the couch and said she was fed up with with her daughter Ihsan's kids, who never left anything in its place.

Bahey listened to her as he took out a strip of aspirin from his gallabiya pocket while standing up. He put the two pills on his tongue and took the earthenware drinking jug from its place next to the television, swigging a mouthful of water and swallowing them. He sat on the other couch and placed his hand with the prayer beads on his bent knee and the left one on the armrest, informing her that Umm Hussein, the greengrocer, had given him a tattered twenty-five piaster note before noon and that he returned it to her son Gaber, who took it and gave him another one. He touched the corner of his mouth with his fingertips.

Nargis asked him if his tooth still hurt and Bahey said, "Yes."

"Then have it pulled."

"It's nothing."

"But if it hurts you . . ."

"Oh, Umm Abduh, I'm not about to have it pulled and all that."

Nargis said everybody did it at the civil servants' hospital, and an hour's pain was better than pain every hour. "Or are you atoning for some sin and have to spend your whole life in pain?" she asked.

"It's not my whole life or anything. It'll probably be a little while and then it will go away by itself."

Nargis went silent as she thought about her teeth, which floated and fell in her mouth without any pain. "My teeth have gone bad on their own," she said. She used to throw them out the window. She continued, "They used to be sound and in perfect condition. The power is late in coming."

"It'll be here."

"I wonder if it's cut at the mosque, too."

"All of Fadlallah Uthman is completely dark."

He said the kids had not shown up; he hadn't seen any of them. But Nargis said that Dalal's son Abdalla was here and Salama was probably dragging his wife along and coming soon.

9

"When did this happen?"

"While you were sleeping."

"And what about Ihsan?"

"Her kids were here, little Nargis and the boy Walid." And she told him that Walid had sat down and demanded, "Give me a shilling, Grandma." Then he grabbed it, slammed the door behind him, and left.

Abu Abduh said, "That kid, with his hair and eye color, reminds me of Shaykh Rashed in the village, the father of the martyred Abd al-Semeeʻ, may he rest in peace. You remember him, Nargis?"

Nargis shifted her weight on the couch and said, "Very well," and she described his torn gallabiya and round skullcap, and how as a girl she used to chase him with Yahya's kids, from the Tanahy's house to Sidi Ali al-Shanabi on the west side of the village.

She said, "He was a sinner, Abu Abduh."

Abu Abduh shook his head and said, "God has His ways."

He told her that after Rashed repented he would stand at the door of Sidi Ali al-Shanabi and whisper into the keyhole, "Ali! Boy! *Salaamu aleikum.* Open up boy, it's me Rashed." Then the door to the mosque, which was always locked from the inside with brass locks, would open wide and Rashed would go in to sleep and the door would close behind him.

Nargis said, "He was from the Labboudi clan, Abu Abduh."

"I know, and I know all his cousins. Their land was by the farthest drainage canal."

"What a world. Abu Abduh, d'you think Rashed is dead?"

"He probably is, who knows?"

Nargis made a sucking noise with her toothless mouth and said, "What's going on with this power?" She was silent for a minute, then said, "Abu Abduh, when I die, I wish you'd put a light bulb in my grave."

"What do you mean?"

"You know, even for just a week."

It was the first time Bahey had heard such talk and he said, "It would blow a fuse, woman."

"Never. Nothing would happen to it."

Bahey grew quiet and reflected that the light bulb might not blow a fuse after all. And he thought to himself, "Really, what would make it burst?" His thoughts turned to the two angels who counted up good deeds and sins and whether it would be proper for them to judge a person under the light of the bulb. He muttered words asking forgiveness from God and scratched his left leg. The topic seemed to him very strange. He left the couch to bring the tea kit: the kerosene burner, the blue teapot, and the cups.

Nargis kept saying that he could get a wire from Abd al-Khaleq the undertaker and buy a light bulb, even if it's only a fifty-watt one like that in the bathroom, and a socket. "It wouldn't even cost fifty piasters, or even forty. You know, just for a week, till I get used to the dark," she said.

Abu Abduh put sugar in the glasses as he said to himself, "What wire and socket?" He thought that the wire, after being put in the grave, would have to be covered over with soil and then the other end would stick out and he'd plug it into the outlet at Abd al-Khaleq's. And of course the humidity would eat at it and anyone could step on it and get electrocuted. They'd die and there'd be a ruckus.

He lit the burner and placed the blue teapot on it, handing her the matchbox. He told her not to lose it this time.

She took it from him and hid it under the armrest, saying hopelessly, "Ihsan's kids are little devils—they never ever leave anything in its place."

Nargis was startled by a movement in the dark, outside the open apartment door. She called out as she gathered up her legs, calling, "Who is it?"

Her brother said, "It's so bright in here!"

Bahey said, "Where've you been?"

"At home." And he sat on the edge of the sofa with his hands in the pockets of his gallabiya.

"You came here and left mother in the dark, Abd al-Reheem?" asked Nargis reproachfully.

He laughed. "As if she knows whether it's light or dark."

The power was out until noon prayers were over at the nearby mosque the next day. Bahey took his slippers from the shelf of the bookcase at the mosque entrance and walked, his short frame in the blazing sun, until he got to Umm Hussein, the greengrocer. He went in through the building door and climbed the few steps, exposing his clean legs and thanking God that the brick had fallen on Umm Hussein and not himself.

When he reached the half-open door of the apartment he spotted Muhammad Effendi al-Rashidi at the other end of the courtyard. When he noticed how tall he was in his striped gallabiya standing on the first step of the inside staircase, he acted quickly and let the hem of his gallabiya fall to his feet and quietly pushed the door open to go in silently, but al-Rashidi heard him and said, "How are you, Bahey?" He lifted the pocket watch to his left eye as he was standing, then raised his face with its big nose, went down the step, and came over. As he adjusted the chain attached to the button hole and let the pocket watch dangle on his chest he said, "How are you doing now, Abu Abdalla?"

"Thanks be to God, Abu Hanan."

Abu Hanan listened and kept looking at him, then put his hand on his shoulder and took him by the open window overlooking the building's shaft and asked him in a low voice about what Umm

Hanan heard from Umm Abdalla: "Is it true you're retired?"

Bahey leaned back against the windowsill and took in the odor of humidity and the chicken coop and smiled as if he was about to talk, then fell silent.

"By God, so it's true," said Abu Hanan.

"It's true, but I filed a complaint."

Abu Hanan went a little pale and moved his head closer, "To who?"

"Those in charge."

"What do you mean?"

Bahey took off his slipper and rubbed the underside of his naked foot on the big toe of the other foot as he explained that it was all a mistake, the government let him go at age sixty instead of sixty-five. "You see, I was appointed as technical staff," he said.

"Technical staff?"

"Why do you think I get unemployment compensation?"

"How much do you get?"

"Twenty percent."

"Comprehensive?"

"No, only basics."

Abu Hanan was surprised and said, "What do you mean?"

Bahey felt nervous when he found him saying "What do you mean?" for the second time, and so soon after the first. He put his slipper back on and wanted to leave; he had been able to maintain the purity of his ablutions since the dawn prayers and now he wanted to go to the bathroom. He moved away from the window and toward the apartment door.

Al-Rashidi caught up with him and said, "But that's very strange, Abu Abdalla."

"Not to worry."

"But what are you going to do?"

"I just told you, Abu Hanan."

"I know you just told me, but that doesn't mean it's not a serious matter."

"Serious how?"

"Like I just said."

"But it's a mistake."

"Are you sure?"

Bahey said yes, because about a year ago they took away his motorcycle and gave him the time sheets and considered him office staff. "I don't know how they totally forgot about this motorcycle thing," he said.

"What do you mean they took it? It's in your custody."

"What is?"

"The motorcycle."

"The commissioner."

"The medical commissioner?"

"Yes."

"What do you mean?"

When Bahey heard this expression for the third time, his round face reddened with frustration and he said, "He's the one who wrote it."

"So it's an official report?"

"It's a piece of paper."

"This piece of paper, what did he write on it?"

Bahey sighed and replied, "He wrote that I had to turn it in."

"Turn what in?"

"Oh brother! The motorcycle."

"All right, all right." He thought for a minute then said, "If that's how it is, what do you say about our project?"

"What project?"

"Our old project, Abu Abduh. The shop."

"What shop?"

"Old man M'gahed's fuul shop."

"What about it?"

"It's over, the man's finished."

"Poor man. Only God is all powerful."

Al-Rashidi said, "That's not the important thing. What matters now is the shop. We have to take it."

"Take it how?"

"Oh brother! Like anyone would."

Al-Rashidi asked him to note that Bahey was now retired, so nothing took up his time. He could get up, perform the dawn prayers, then open up the shop and stay there until al-Rashidi returned from work.

"I'll pray the afternoon prayer and have a bite, then take over from you. We've got nothing to be ashamed of," said al-Rashidi.

"And the money?"

"What money?"

"The money we'll need to buy supplies."

Al-Rashidi said, "It's a negligible amount, and if we put our heads together you'll see that all we need is a can of whitewash to paint the walls and front, two or three wooden shelves, and a reasonable quantity of supplies. After that, it'll be only a year and I'll retire too and we'll work the same shift because business will have grown by then."

Bahey said importantly, "Generally, commercial activity *is* profitable."

"Very. And besides, think about this . . . " and al-Rashidi began counting off on his fingers and answering his own questions: "The size of the shop? Very suitable. The location? Perfect. The distance? A stone's throw away. The rent? A few piasters. What else is there, Abu Abdalla?"

Abu Abdalla watched each finger Abu Hanan counted off give way to the next, raised his bald head, and looked at Muhammad Effendi al-Rashidi's nose. Al-Rashidi placed his hand on his shoulder and returned him to his place by the half-open apartment door, asking him to leave it up to God. He alerted him to the fact that the most important thing now was not to tell anyone about the matter, especially Umm Abdalla. He stressed the point, "Abu Abdalla?"

"Of course not, Abu Hanan."

"All right then, *salaamu aleikum.*" He lifted the hem of his gallabiya and began to descend the stairs.

"*Aleikum al-salaam.*"

Bahey opened the door and looked at Nargis, who was sitting looking out the window, her hand on her cheek. He went into the inner room, took off his gallabiya, flung it on the bed, and went up to his government uniform, which was hanging on the window latch. He put his hand in the outside pocket and took out the pack of cigarettes and matches. He stood on his tiptoes and saw Hagg Mahmoud the coal dealer sitting on a bench on this side of Fadlallah Uthman, and old man M'gahed dozing at the front of the shop by the big fuul urn. Lighting the cigarette, he quickly headed to the bathroom.

He closed the door firmly, lifted his undershirt to his chest, and dropped his pants. He sat finishing his business and smoking, running a match through his shadow reflected in the water on the floor. After he had relieved himself, he leaned over and threw the match into the round opening, shook his head, and said, "You crazy man, Abu Hanan."

During the afternoon prayers, Hagg Mahmoud the coal dealer came up to him from the rear of the mosque and told him that Fathi Emad, a lawyer and the district's candidate for parliament, was meeting voters at the suq grounds right after the evening prayers and suggested that he give him a copy of his complaint.

Bahey was surprised that Hagg Mahmoud knew about the complaint and looked at him silently, then said, "You don't say?"

"Believe me, Abu Abdalla. He's the government candidate."

He stood with his short, full frame in his sooty gallabiya and spoke in his gravelly voice, his wool cap slipping off his short white hair. Bahey moved away quickly down Fadlallah Uthman. After the evening prayers, he folded the copy of his complaint into a colored air mail envelope and stuffed it into his inside jacket pocket, setting off from Fadlallah Uthman accompanied by Hagg Mahmoud the coal dealer, Abd al-Reheem, and Muhammad Effendi al-Rashidi. The whole way there he walked a couple of steps behind them, smiling in embarrassment. At one point he kicked a stone with his right foot and almost fell.

When they reached the suq grounds, they found the chairs arranged in a big circle with an empty table in the middle covered with a tablecloth and surrounded by four chairs for the candidate and his aides. Muhammad Effendi al-Rashidi quickly told them to take seats in the front row near the table. Ma'allim Sobhi was standing outside, his eyes watching the street expectantly. As for the coffee boy, he was in a state of visible excitement as he placed glasses of hot karkadeh before them.

Most of the seats were still empty. Bahey seemed embarrassed as he drank the karkadeh, but suddenly something crossed his mind, and he leaned over Hagg Mahmoud and whispered in his ear, "How did you know, Hagg?"

"Know about what, Abu Abdalla?"

"About this thing."

"What thing?"

"About the story of this complaint."

"You mean your retirement?"

Bahey shook his head imperceptibly. Hagg Mahmoud whispered that al-Rashidi—Abu Hanan—had told him everything,

"And we're family after all, Abu Abdalla," he said, his hoarse voice trembling.

"Right," said Bahey.

He threw al-Rashidi a sharp glance out of the corner of his eye, hating him and the short hairs that hung out of his disgusting nostrils. True, all his life he never felt at ease with him, but that feeling waxed and waned depending on the circumstances. And now he was in a state where he would rather put up with blindness than deal with al-Rashidi.

The number of attendees grew and the noise level increased as people waited for the tardy candidate. Bahey began busying himself thinking about all the faults he knew about al-Rashidi. The first was when they were young and were going to the mosque to pray one day. While they were kneeling in prayer to God Almighty, a silver ten piaster coin rolled out of the pocket of one of the praying men and came to a rest in front of them. When they prostrated themselves before God he saw al-Rashidi's palm land right over the coin, and after they uttered "Glory be to God" the required three times and straightened up and lifted their hands from the floor, the coin had miraculously disappeared. Later, in the courtyard of the apartment building, before each went on his way, Bahey stared at the top pocket of al-Rashidi's gallabiya, looking for an imprint of the heavy coin in the thin fabric.

He awoke from his reverie to the clamor made by the entourage of the candidate, who came from the Nile road seated on the interlocked arms of two men. They placed him on the chair carefully. He was panting in his three-piece suit, a colorful kerchief peeking out of his front suit pocket. Bahey noticed that the man was stocky with silver hair, his flushed face was leaning on his chest, and his mouth was slightly twisted. Shaykh Ali al-Sunni, the mosque's preacher, was sitting on his right, smiling, with his kind face and big black beard. By this time, all the seats were taken and there were many people standing. He also noticed that the candidate was now breathing normally. He opened two gray eyes and Bahey was surprised by his loud voice as he said, "Good evening, men." Bahey looked right and left and chuckled to himself softly, then sat silent and still.

A group of aides were circulating among the voters to make sure that everyone had had some karkadeh. Bahey noticed that Muhammad Effendi al-Rashidi had asked for another glass and drank it with evident delight, and that the candidate had closed his eyes again and tilted his heavy head, his hands on his cheek, leaning on the table. Bahey felt repelled by al-Rashidi's greediness, and realized that every group of men were talking among themselves. He started thinking that the purpose of the meeting was only to drink karkadeh, but he gathered from the conversations that they were waiting for the leaflets to arrive from the printing house so they could be distributed. Mahmoud the coal dealer suggested that Abu Abdalla give the complaint to the candidate, and when he didn't answer him, he made the same suggestion to Muhammad Effendi al-Rashidi who replied, "What, he still hasn't given it to him?"

He turned to Bahey and said, "What's going on, Abu Abdalla? Go up to him."

But Bahey ignored him completely, while Abd al-Reheem heard all this and put out his hand. "Hand it over, Bahey." Bahey turned to him and when he saw his insistence, he handed him the envelope and said, "The man's asleep, Abd al-Reheem."

Yet the candidate was not completely asleep because his cheek slipped off his palm while his eyes were still closed. His wrist was on the table and he kept opening and closing his fingers. When his fingertips touched Shaykh Ali al-Sunni's beard, he held on to it and caressed it gently and pulled at it, while the Shaykh's face leaned toward the tabletop, taking on a pensive expression. At that point, a man burst through the crowd holding a stack of twined paper to his chest and called out, "The leaflets, sir."

The candidate came to attention with a start and let go of the beard as he barked, "What are you waiting for? Hand it out to the men, it's made for them." He turned to Shaykh Ali, "Isn't that right, honorable shaykh?" The shaykh smiled without commenting.

Bahey took a leaflet and saw the faded picture at the top, compared it to the candidate and saw that it resembled him. His eyes ran over the writing about the services he'd done for the district, and looked up as the candidate held up a leaflet and yelled, "By God, by God, if I was a voter I'd vote for this man!"

He burst out laughing and others joined in.

When Abd al-Reheem noticed that they were approaching the candidate to carry him away, he ran up to him and stuffed the complaint into his pocket as Mahmoud the coal man followed and called out that this decent man, pointing to Bahey, would guarantee him all of Fadlallah Uthman's votes. Bahey saw the candidate as he shook his head, as if moved while sitting on the interlocked arms. Before they turned on their way to the big, open car he spotted the candidate's two small testicles squeezed into a corner of his crotch, and part of his skinny legs exposed to reveal his socks.

They were silent until they reached Fadlallah Uthman. Then Mahmoud the coal man said, "I'm optimistic about this man."

Abd al-Reheem, walking with his hands in his gallabiya pockets, said, "Let's wait and see if he's going to win or not. And even if he wins, he needs to come for another meeting."

Muhammad Effendi al-Rashidi commented, "He's the government candidate, Abd al-Reheem. Did you see the car he was in?"

Bahey ignored al-Rashidi's comments and said to Abd al-Reheem, "He was sitting there sleeping."

"He was tired, Abu Abdalla. He's been making the rounds all day," said Mahmoud.

"So he plays with Shaykh Ali al-Sunni's beard?"

"What are you talking about?" said al-Rashidi.

Bahey stopped and said angrily, "Yes, he did. He took hold of his beard and was pulling it."

"That didn't happen."

"Come on now, we all saw him holding the man's beard and pulling it," said Abd al-Reheem.

"You mean when he thought it was a glass of tea?"

"A glass of tea?"

"Yes, what'd you think?"

Bahey thought for a bit and said, "What brought the glass on the table near Shaykh Ali's beard which is on his face?" When they fell silent, he added, "And where did a glass of tea come from if everybody was drinking karkadeh?"

And without looking this way or that, he smiled as if to say, "You ignorant sons of bitches!"

Nobody could dissuade al-Bahey Uthman from the path he'd embarked on. All night he'd draft and write complaints explaining how the Postal Service had wronged him by depriving him of five full years of service. No matter what time Nargis would open her eyes as she lay sleeping on her side in the middle of the night, she would see him sitting at the low, round table, writing without pause, a pile of complaints and copies of complaints stacked up on the couch near his left shoulder, while plain and lined sheets of paper—some crumpled, some clean—and carbon copies were strewn all around him on the rug.

In the beginning, Bahey would write with some concentration, sufficing with an explanation of the injustice that had befallen him and the dire consequences that would ensue if the government did not set the matter right. He was confident that it would do something because the error that had occurred was crystal clear. He was appointed as technical staff, and all the official papers proved this, thus his retirement age had to be set at sixty-five. Erroneously considering him office staff and ending his service at age sixty would not only deprive him of his job and a salary for five full years as was his right, but would also deprive him of ten pounds (a two-pound bonus each year), which would have increased his pension when his real term of service ended at age sixty-five.

Truth be told, Bahey spent long nights clearly laying out the problem so that any official could understand it, which filled him with pride at his abilities that came through at a time of need. He closed the door and sat facing Nargis on the other sofa, reading her the complaint slowly in a voice she found unfamiliar. When he read it once again, standing this time, his demeanor changed even more, which set her mind wandering far away from what she was listening to. He began by uttering God's name and then a cordial greeting, getting right into the matter. He wrote that he could not believe this had happened to him after forty-two years of service, during which he received not a single probation or disciplinary action. Therefore, he requested that the injustice be remedied and the five years that were his right returned to him, like all his colleagues in the technical staff. He then ended the complaint by stating that he reserved the right to demand compensation if the injustice persisted. It was an expression that had stuck with him because of its legal nature and because he'd run across it in many of the complaints he'd seen. He delivered this statement in a slow admonishing tone, which made Nargis listen up and filled her with fear.

Yet the hopes he'd nurtured didn't last for long. The reply soon came explaining that a few years ago he'd been transferred from technical to office staff after the medical commissioner had decided when renewing his driver's license that his eyesight had weakened. He was no longer able to drive the motorcycle and collect letters from mailboxes, and that he then became responsible for time sheets, and he had signed the transfer at the time, confirming his acceptance of this desk job.

The reply stunned him and made him alter the content of his complaint so that it read like a clear call for help. He sent tens of protests to the Postal Service, the ministry, the trade union, the attorney general, and the Arab Socialist Union. His last letter was addressed to President Gamal Abd al-Nasser, informing him that when they would sort the mail before the 1952 Revolution they would recognize the pamphlets of the Free Officers (they used the same envelopes) and wouldn't report them, but gave them to their colleagues the mail carriers to distribute without the knowledge of officials. He hoped that the president would appreciate that he was one of those loyal to the revolution and had a hand in its success. But while he was expectantly waiting for a response, Abd al-Nasser died suddenly.

The problem worsened. Nargis and the kids talked to him, telling him not to worry and that it was time he took a rest. "And besides, the difference is minimal. You can make it up by saving on commuting fees." Bahey would nod in agreement with some embarrassment, but in his heart he was convinced that he couldn't accept this situation at all. He used to begin his day by shaving in front of the mirror, looking at his ruddy baby face and beautiful eyes and arranging his small, white-flecked moustache. Then he would put on his brown suit and shiny necktie, pick up his folder containing several copies of his first complaint, and head to the Postal Service. But the negative response made him lose his energy completely. He now began his day by putting on his clothes hurriedly, then picking up the enlarged folder with its dog-eared papers, and heading out hastily without shaving.

He returned at the end of the day, exhausted, from no one knew where. Nargis didn't see him sleep at all, at night or by day. With time, he completely abandoned his old habits. He started wearing any old trousers and shirts belonging to him or one of the kids, whatever fell into his hands, which made each of them keep a close watch on their clothes. What's more, he started to openly scorn Nargis's concern for other people's feelings and cared not a whit for what this or that one said. And he completely stopped going to the mosque.

Al-Bahey Uthman lifted his right foot as far as he could. He climbed into the pickup truck and sat beside Nargis at the end of the wooden bench, under the stained, torn plastic tarpaulin. He was wearing an old brown suit and shiny necktie, his right hand holding firmly onto the vertical steel bar and his left hand clutching his prayer beads and fare, while Nargis, wearing her heavy dark dress and black silk head cover, leaned her head out to watch the road; he moved his knees away from the aisle for passengers climbing aboard.

The truck was full and began to move, men standing in the back holding onto the plastic ceiling. It moved slowly, swaying under the weight and stopping numerous times on account of all the traffic, piles of trash, and pedestrians. When it crossed the ramp, the fender fell off and got stuck on the railroad tracks. The crash hurt Bahey's rear end. "The truck's on the flaps," he said.

The man standing to his right laughed and looked at his neighbor. Bahey noticed right away and lifted his hairless head, smiling quizzically with his exhausted eyes. "It's called the rim, not the flaps," the man clarified. This puzzled Bahey and preoccupied him for the rest of the trip. When they disembarked and crossed the street, Nargis opened her toothless mouth, "What were you saying when the people laughed at you in the truck?"

He stopped on the sidewalk and asked her angrily, "Wasn't there something called the flaps a long time ago?"

"What? What do you mean, 'was there something called the flaps a long time ago'?"

"Then where'd I get this word from?"

"What are you talking about, Abu Abduh? Do you mean the wool cap with the earflaps that the Postal Service used to issue you with the winter coat, before you retired?"

He contemplated her a bit then continued walking silently.

She added, "We still have one of them."

"In the apartment?"

"I could've sworn I saw it when I was tidying up the closet the other day."

She stopped in Qatr al-Nada in front of the house looking out onto Fadlallah Uthman. "While I'm dressed, I'll check up on Mother Hanem and get you the saw you wanted from Abd al-Reheem."

"Abd al-Fattah who?" he said.

"What's going on, man? I said Abd al-Reheem, my brother."

She pushed open the closed wooden door, stepped down, and walked into the long hallway. "Anyone home?" she called.

"Come in, Auntie," cried Dalal from the inside.

"Come in, Umm Abdalla," said her brother as he left the big room.

"How's mother, Abd al-Reheem?"

"Sprightly as a monkey."

"Better than yesterday?"

"Much."

He accompanied her to the small room at the end of the covered courtyard, followed by the boy, Abdalla. The rest of the kids were sleeping in the dark, hardly visible in the corner of the bed. "Get up, Hanem. Your daughter's here," said the boy.

"It's Nargis, Ma," said Abd al-Reheem, elbowing the boy.

"Come in, dear."

"No, you stay sleeping. I'll sit with the kids outside."

Nargis sat in the big room and Dalal made tea. They drank it and chatted, and when she got up to leave Abd al-Reheem went along carrying the saw.

She opened the door and went in. It was hot. All the lights were on in the apartment and the windows were closed. Bahey was sitting on the living room sofa in his underwear in front of the turned on television, the woolen cap covering his head all the way down to his eyebrows. The wide brim, with its small buttonholes that fit into the collar of a coat to ward off the winter rains, was around his neck.

Nargis thumped her chest with one hand as she sat on the edge of the other sofa, cupping her chin with the other hand in a gesture of perplexity. "Oh my goodness," she uttered.

"What are you wearing on your head? The weather's steaming hot," said Abd al-Reheem, standing by the door carrying the saw. Bahey was silent, relief in his eyes. His head leaned a little to the side and disappeared into the cap, his right hand in his lap and his left extended on his bent knee. The old prayer beads were hanging from the fingers of his clasped hand.

26

In the light of day, on one side of the dusty uphill road in the burial grounds in the Sidi Omar graveyard, Nargis sat on the earth weeping, surrounded by her daughters and the hired mourning women of Fadlallah Uthman in their grubby black gallabiyas. When al-Bahey Uthman passed her by, carried in his wooden coffin that was covered by a cloth with a faded print design, she lifted her face where the tears had dried and cried out in reproach, "So you've gone and done it, Abu Abdalla?"

3

IT WAS SUMMER, and the red dates had sprouted. Nargis was alone, al-Bahey Uthman was at work, Abdalla was at school, and the kids were playing on the roof. She was combing her long parted hair, her bronze-colored face ruddy and warm, wincing every time the wooden comb got stuck in her thick, dark locks.

Abd al-Reheem arrived suddenly, surprising her, and said hello. He dragged the two large baskets into the room and sat on the couch resting and letting his sweat dry off. She gathered her hair and started asking him about the village, but Abd al-Reheem went out to Fadlallah Uthman and then to Qatr al-Nada, walking in his country gallabiya and new shoes until he reached Nile Street, and stood with his big frame on the edge of the river.

He watched the girls washing pots at the bottom of the stone steps and the boys fishing. He noticed that each boy was holding a thin stick about fifty inches long, and that the fish coming out of the water were tiny, shivering and shiny in the sunlight. Abd al-Reheem stepped forward, descended the wet stone steps, and asked the nearest boy, "What are you fishing with, pal?"

"With a hook," said the boy.

"I mean, with what bait."

The boy opened his palm to reveal a small, yellow ball.

"This?"

"Yes."

"It's a paste."

"Wheat or corn?"

"A paste, I said, but it's greasy," said the boy, as he pulled strongly on the line, but it came out empty.

Abd al-Reheem looked out with his wide eyes to the surface of the river, wrinkled by the soft breeze. After he'd had enough of watching the boys and the calm, clean buildings on the other side, he went back up the wet stone steps, hiking up the hem of his gallabiya, and crossed the road to the corner of Hawwa Alley. He slowed down in front of Rabie', the fishing pole seller, and saw the cluster of thin poles lying at the store entrance, and then returned to Fadlallah Uthman.

Al-Bahey Uthman had returned from the post office, taken off his uniform and fez, and put on his gallabiya. Nargis had braided her hair and tied a kerchief over her head. Abdalla had come back from school and stood with his brother Salama and their little sister Ihsan, each munching on a small roll in their hands, watching their mother as she pulled back the sheets on the four poster bed and put the small earthenware jar of spicy, aged cheese, jug of ghee, and container of honey on it. She picked leaves of clover off the homemade cheese that filled the copper colander and asked Bahey to put an empty basket on top of the wardrobe. She took some heavy country pancakes laden with ghee out of another basket and put them on the cover of the big brass pot, setting aside the basket with its remaining loaves of bread and small rolls made with whole milk, which reminded Bahey of the smell of the countryside as he stood on the couch with his short, clean frame, placing the empty basket on top of the wardrobe. When Abd al-Reheem came in, Bahey stepped down and embraced him.

"Welcome back, Abd al-Reheem."

"And how are you, Bahey?"

"Fine, fine. Where'd you go?"

"Just to the waterfront and back."

"Welcome back."

"Thank you. How are you doing, Abdalla?"

"Fine," said Abdalla without turning to look at his uncle.

Nargis turned off the burner and placed the big, round, copper tray on the low eating table. She put out the large platter of rice and the china soup tureen, and a pair of the fried chickens her mother Hanem sent from the village. "How's mother, Abd al-Reheem?" she inquired.

"She says hello."

"And Grandmother Aziza?"

"Sprightly as a monkey."

"And Uncle Abd al-Aziz?"

"He's good."

"Does he still have heartburn?" said Bahey between mouthfuls.

"Sometimes, and other times he feels fine."

"When we go to the village next time we'll take him some of those fizzing tablets, they're really good here."

"What fizzing tablets?" asked Abd al-Reheem.

"For heartburn," explained Bahey.

"Why not?" said Abd al-Reheem, thinking about the long wooden stick with a coarse broom brush at the end of it he'd seen at the entrance to the house. "Whose broomstick is that in the courtyard?" he asked.

"It's ours," said Nargis.

"Why do you leave it out there?"

"It's too long for the room. Why are you asking, Abd al-Reheem?" wondered Nargis.

"I want to make a fishing pole out of it."

"What fishing pole, boy? You're coming to Cairo to find work or go fishing?"

"Fishing pole?! That thing would go out halfway into the river," said Abdalla.

"Did you bring the appointment letter with you or did you forget?" Bahey asked Abd al-Reheem.

"I've got it," he said, then he sat eating silently.

In the evening, Abd al-Reheem busied himself with turning the broomstick into a fishing pole, with half of it extending outside the room because it was so long, altogether a bit more than sixteen feet. He bought the biggest hook he could find at Rabie' the fishing pole seller's, a lead weight, and a sturdy cord, which he tied to the edge of the stick after carefully removing the broom head as Nargis had instructed him, so she could use it when she needed to. Bahey, with his fair ruddy face, wavy dark hair, and beautiful eyes, sat on the sofa sleepily watching him and smoking his hand-rolled cigarette. Abdalla got up and got his small fishing pole from next to the wardrobe. "Use this one, it's better, Uncle," he said to Abd al-Reheem.

Abd al-Reheem looked at the thin reed and said, "What's this?"

"It's a fishing pole."

"The kind to use with paste?"

"And worms, too."

"It's no good."

"They're two different things," Bahey commented.

"Suit yourself," said Abdalla. "But when the kids laugh at you, remember that I warned you."

"Be quiet, kid, be quiet," said Abd al-Reheem.

"How could that kid ever be quiet?" Bahey said sarcastically, yawning.

Nargis adjusted the teapot on the burner and said, "But it's true, Abd al-Reheem. Everybody uses those small fishing poles."

Abd al-Reheem stopped attaching the lead weight and said, "What are you talking about, Nargis? It's a not a stream, it's a river for God's sake." He tied the round cork, gathered the cord around the long stick and parked it outside the room, then he went to sleep.

When they woke up in the morning, they returned the mattress Abd al-Reheem and the kids had slept on to its place above the other mattress on the high bed, and had their breakfast of pancakes, cheese, honey, and tea. Nargis divided one of the country-style pancakes into equal pieces and with each piece added a bit of homemade cheese and some rolls, put her head kerchief on, and went around sharing the food with her neighbors. When she came back, Bahey was coming out of the bathroom, making a clanging noise with the wooden clogs after he'd washed up and started to get ready for the Friday prayer, while Abd al-Reheem had gone out, carrying on his shoulder the longest fishing pole the street of Fadlallah Uthman had ever seen, Abdalla following him in gallabiya and sandals.

Abd al-Reheem descended the wet stone steps and moved left, inspecting the area underfoot. He parked the pole, hitched up the hem of his gallabiya and tied it to his waist. Using both hands, he picked up a large rock from the riverbank silt and threw it aside, then quickly snatched up the large red fishing worms that were trying to flee. He encircled the worms with the silt to trap them but keep them alive, and kept one in his left hand, clapping on it with his right hand until it became lifeless.

He then tore off a piece of the worm and attached it to the hook, gave his leather slippers to Abdalla who was lying on the bank, and waded into the water, wetting his long pants. He threw in the line as hard as he could and stood watching the float.

No sooner had the long, uneven line made it into the water than it caught the attention of all the kids, and a sense of watchfulness and worry descended over the riverbank.

The Friday prayer and its long sermon ended at the mosque above the riverbank, and Abd al-Reheem was still standing looking at the float with watchful eyes until it started to bob up and down. He became alert and held onto the line, waiting for the right moment, then suddenly pulled on it as hard as he could. The cord twisted in the air and caused a drizzle as it came nearer, dragging a dark catch. As soon as it faced Abd al-Reheem, it scratched him violently in the nose, fluttering and flapping its wings caught in the cord, for it was a sparrow that became ensnared in the hook while flying overhead. Abd al-Reheem was stunned and did not understand, he thought the thing had come out of the water. Everyone watching was taken aback as they watched him stumble and fall as he made his way up the bank, far from the steps, still holding on to the long raised line. The kids ran behind him as the hitched sparrow tugged on the cord, raising it high above everyone, and it became a large procession that made its way to the big bridge.

Abdalla returned to Fadlallah Uthman and tossed his uncle's slippers behind the door. "What's that, Abdalla?" asked Nargis.

"Uncle Abd al-Reheem's slippers."

"So where is he, boy?"

"I don't know."

"Oh my God! He must've drowned!"

"He didn't drown."

"So why'd you bring his slippers, Abdalla?"

"He's the one who left them and ran."

Bahey stood up. "Ran?" he asked.

"And everyone was running after him."

"Why?" screamed Nargis. "What'd he do, Abdalla? Say something!"

"His line caught a sparrow."

"Oh my God! A sparrow?" said Bahey, his face turning pale.

"Yes, from the river."

"What are you talking about?"

"But it's a blue sparrow."

"And where is he now?"

"He ran toward the police station."

The hesitation was obvious on Bahey's face. "The police station?" He looked at his son with angry eyes. "You dirty son of a bitch!" he yelled.

"What're you cursing *me* for?" said Abdalla as he got ready to flee.

Bahey ran out to Fadlallah Uthman, hitching up his gallabiya, and Nargis quickly put on her face veil and black wrap and followed suit. When they found him after this first fishing expedition, he was exhausted in his wet gallabiya and bare feet. His face was scratched and his hair disheveled after he'd lost his new skullcap, so that Nargis didn't recognize him until she peered closer to identify him. They took him back to Fadlallah Uthman and closed their door to keep out prying eyes.

Abd al-Reheem washed up and lay down with his eyes closed. He didn't calm down until Nargis made him a cup of tea and rubbed his forehead with a lime cut in half. Only then did he open his eyes and look around him. Then he burst out crying.

When he came to, after they removed the stone from his right kidney, he saw her in front of him in the tight, white coat and the cap pinned into her blond hair. She smiled at him with her light-colored eyes and left. The second time, she stretched out her hand and removed his clothes. She changed the bandaging and cleaned his bare stomach, and when she was pulling down his gallabiya over his legs, the side of her pinky finger gently brushed against his sleeping member, and she left. With every new dressing, his whole body anticipated that touch that he would never forget. When she didn't do it again, he realized that she was bashful because he was eyeing her. So he decided to relieve her of this shyness, and his tactic was to make her think that he was oblivious when she changed his bandaging, completely occupied by other things, so he would stare out the window or close his eyes completely. But she would finish and pull down the gallabiya over his hairy legs.

But before she left, she would unhurriedly look at his wheat-colored face and brown eyes and the expression of docile gratitude he would greet her with. She recognized that he came from a good, well-off family. His sister Nargis was young and beautiful, visiting him every day with her gold bracelets, earrings, and necklace, laden with bags of fruit that she would distribute to the patients and nurses. And her husband, Bahey Effendi, had a dignified bearing as he came in with his wool suit, patterned brown necktie, and fez. He would sit silently on the edge of the bed with his shiny, wavy hair, rolling a cigarette from his patterned tin box, looking at her with his ruddy face and alluring eyes.

Her name was Afkar. And she knew, as her co-workers knew, that Abd al-Reheem had deposited a large sum of money in the hospital safe that he said was rent from his land (but truthfully, it was his share of the price of a piece of land they sold because it fell outside their registered plots), and she also knew that he was a government employee. She would give him a bold look and he would look away immediately. And when Nargis would visit him and ask him about the wound, he would say he's fine, thanks to the lady doctor.

Once Nargis asked him, "Which doctor are you talking about, Abd al-Reheem?"

"The one who changes my bandaging."

"That fair, pretty one?"

"Yes, she's kind and has a really light touch."

"That's the nurse, boy!"

"He laughed and said, "Really?"

"Yes, aren't you talking about Afkar?"

"Yes, that's her."

"She's the nurse for the whole ward."

Nargis didn't waste any time. She wanted to get him away from his current girlfriend, 'Basima a la Mode,' at any price, so she spoke to Afkar and got her address, which was close to the shrine of Sidi Hassan Abu Tartur. So, barely a few weeks after Abd al-Reheem left the hospital, he became engaged to Afkar.

At first, when Nargis told him that Afkar had agreed to the engagement, he was not convinced, were it not for that old touch that he always remembered and then get an erection. The only thing that would prevent him from continuing was the wound in his abdomen. It was the touch that was their secret that convinced him of her consent to be engaged. Over time, he accepted the fact that her skin was rosy, that her eyes were green-yellow, and that her hair was blond. But it was the matter of her thin bosom yet large behind and full legs that gave him pause, with a vague feeling of distress and resignation.

In spite of this, the engagement and the signing of the marriage contract took place on the same day, and they agreed to hold the wedding party a year later. Abd al-Reheem went with Bahey to the Egyptian Textile Company and bought an olive-colored wool suit with fine white pinstripes, a white shirt, and a tie. He watched Bahey as he sat on the couch fixing the knot on the tie around his bent knee, then Abd al-Reheem kneeled down in front of him with his shirt collar upturned and put it on. His mother, Hanem, came from the village with her slender frame and radiant face, wearing her black crepe georgette veil. She sat with her characteristic pride, hiding her admiration of Afkar's beauty.

Afkar was wearing the customary gifts of gold from her fiancé: a heavy gold bracelet in the shape of a snake, earrings, and the engagement ring. In the corner next to Bahey sat Abd al-Rahman, the village chief and Abd al-Reheem's cousin, who had come in his white Mercedes with Uncle Abd al-Aziz Abu Shanab of the angry face and slightly crossed eye. After the signing of the marriage contract, Abu Shanab insisted on going home to the village that night and wouldn't hear of spending the night.

Afkar noticed that Abd al-Reheem was a little afraid of her and so she encouraged him. She would hold his hand while explaining something to him, or touch him lightly as she passed by with that behind of hers, which had a special place in his thoughts. In truth, he tried more than once to be bold and touch her, but his powers totally failed him. He was overwhelmed by the color of her hair, eyes, and skin and her commanding feminine voice. When she stood talking to him in her revealing housedress, showing him the see-through nightgowns her uncle had sent her from the Gulf, he kept looking at them and listening to her, feeling really sad.

He noticed that she closed the old suitcase and bent down in front of him, pushing it under the wardrobe. When she straightened, she moved her cheek close to his mouth and lowered her eyelids, her eyes contemplating the bed sheets in a mysterious way. Then he remembered her finger brushing past his member in the hospital and thought to kiss her but she moved her cheek away a little, and he felt too embarrassed to move his lips forward to reach her, so he found it easier to extend his hand down to her housedress and lift it up. Afkar blushed and struggled with him to let go of her housedress and stormed out of the room, and he called in sick the next day and didn't go to work. From that day on, Afkar was careful not be alone with him anywhere or turn her back to him under any circumstances.

Spring was over, and Nargis rented the house that looked out onto the beginning of Fadlallah Uthman for Abd al-Reheem, who had completely stopped wearing the wool suit he had bought for the wedding and had folded up the white shirt with its starched collar and stashed them both in the closet. When he returned from work, he would take off his work-issued summer suit and put on the country vest with its large pockets that held his wallet and papers underneath one of the gallabiyas fashioned by al-Ghamrini, the village tailor without peer in all of Cairo. Afkar liked the fabric of these gallabiyas when he visited her at her parents' house and found that they suited him.

When he went over one evening to pick her and her younger sister up to go to the outdoor theater, three days after it had opened, he found her wearing a navy-blue dress with a thin white belt, her blond hair in a pony tail that rested on her left breast. She looked at him and said, "Aren't you coming?"

"Where?"

"What do you mean 'where'? To the movies!"

"Of course I am. I've got the tickets right here," and he reached into his top pocket and pulled them out.

"Then why didn't you get dressed?"

Abd al-Reheem looked at his clean, ironed gallabiya and shoes with the laces neatly tied and chuckled, "Well, I'm not exactly undressed."

"No, I mean a suit, pants, and a shirt—anything else."

"Why wear a suit? I'm not traveling anywhere."

Afkar's mother, who had been going back and forth through the living room, stopped and said, "What's going on, Afkar?"

"What do you mean what's going on, Mama?" And she stood up so her pony tail slipped from her left breast and disappeared behind her. "There's no way I can go out with him looking like this."

"It's just a few blocks away."

"So we're not going to the movies?" said the younger sister.

Afkar sat down. "We can't." She thought for a minute and said, "Give me those tickets," and she took them from him.

"Oh, please let him come with us," said the young girl.

Afkar studied the tickets and smiled. "And you got floor seats, too?" She extended her hand to him with one ticket. "Go on and get dressed and catch up with us. I'm only going for her sake," she said moving her head in the direction of her younger sister.

"You're being unreasonable, Afkar," said her mother.

"Mama, the cinema has continuous screenings, so he won't miss anything. And besides, there are things he has to know, starting now. I can never go out with him while he's wearing a gallabiya, ever. And besides, he's not upset." She turned to him. "Abd al-Reheem, are you upset by what I'm saying?"

"Not at all."

"Okay then, go change and catch up with us."

As he approached the door, the young girl caught up to him and said, "Hurry up, so you can come and watch the movie with us."

He left feeling very embarrassed by that little girl.

"You were really unreasonable, Afkar," said the mother to her daughter, who was adjusting her dress in front of the mirror.

"Mama, I can't go out with him when he's wearing a gallabiya." She yelled, "I won't be humiliated!"

"Girl, he's inexperienced. You have to teach him."

Abd al-Reheem didn't change and didn't go to the cinema— he spent the evening with his sister and her husband and their kids instead. He never said anything bad about Afkar in front of Nargis so she would not hate her. By day he'd hang around the hospital and in the evenings he would want to go see her as usual, then he would remember her younger sister and his embarrassment in front of her and he couldn't bring himself to go. He thought, "What does she mean, a suit? I'm not like Bahey, my sister's husband. God, what a pain."

Nargis noticed that there was something going on and said to him, "Abd al-Reheem, don't stop visiting them, she's your wife after all."

So he dug up the shirt and put it on with the suit and went to see her during her shift in the hospital. Afkar greeted him nicely in front of her co-workers and didn't ask him why he hadn't come to the cinema, though her eyes stopped at his rumpled shirt collar and she whispered, "You should iron your shirt," with a big smile in her light-colored eyes.

He started visiting her house with the gallabiya again, and she'd say, "Fine, since we're not going out."

His mother-in-law grabbed every opportunity to goad him, "You know how girls are, they like to show off their fiancés."

Or she would try to win him over. "Don't be upset with Afkar, you know, a doctor asked to marry her and she refused." And she would add, "She'll mature when she goes out into the world. She's still young, you know."

The second time he visited her in the hospital, he was wearing his government-issued yellow suit because he left work and went to the hospital with Nargis and her son Abdalla, who had jumped from the top of a high grotto in the Fish Gardens and got caught in the chin by the barbed wire. It dug into his skin and swung him left and right until he fell, leaving a deep, bloody wound.

Afkar welcomed Nargis and went about her tasks in complete silence, but at the first chance she got, she turned to Abd al-Reheem as he stood in the yellow suit with its shiny brass buttons and said, "What do you think you're wearing?"

"I came here straight from the office."

He didn't see her again until Nargis took him to Afkar's house, on the occasion of her uncle's return from his sojourn in the Gulf. She thought what was happening was a kind of girlish silliness, but al-Bahey Uthman had a different opinion, because the issue of taking care of his external appearance had been a natural disposition in him ever since he realized its importance. It was that care that impressed itself upon everyone he met from the village, so that they really could not tell the difference between the way he dressed and the way city folk dressed. True, he didn't wear his brown suit except on special occasions, but afterward he wouldn't just leave it lying around, but would give it a good once-over with the coarse lint brush, hang it up, and cover it with half of an old gallabiya. As for the work-issued winter or summer suit, he wouldn't put it on until he'd heated up the iron on the flaming burner, sprayed the suit with water, and ironed it, and then he'd put it on over a shirt and tie after he'd buffed its buttons. Before he went to sleep, he had to prepare the shoe polish and soft brush, clean his shoes, and carefully put them away.

That was his way, which he never changed, and that led him to realize from the beginning that someone who didn't know how to take care of his appearance wouldn't suit Afkar. So, when Nargis went with Abd al-Reheem on their way to re-establish contact on the pretext of greeting the uncle returning from the Gulf, Bahey waited until they moved off and then said in an audible voice, "Ha, you can piss on my grave if they get back together."

Nargis and Abd al-Reheem sat surrounded by the whole family. The younger sister said, "Why don't you come around any-more, Uncle?" Abd al-Reheem patted her on the back silently. Uncle Abbas came in after he'd finished the evening prayer in the bedroom, and Afkar's mother introduced him, "Hagg Abbas, my brother and the bride's uncle."

"Welcome, welcome," said Nargis.

Afkar's mother added, "Nargis, Abdalla's mother and Mr. Abd al-Reheem's sister."

Abbas sat cross-legged on the couch and leaned toward them in his white gallabiya with a packet of Marlboros peeking out of his top pocket, smiling, and said, "Greetings to you all."

They talked little during tea, and when they were done, they fell completely silent. Afkar's mother went into the kitchen and came back with an apple she cut in half and gave one half to Nargis and one to Abd al-Reheem, and said, "I swear it's the last one."

Abd al-Reheem ate his half and after he gave thanks, he heard Nargis wiping her strong, white teeth and saying, "It tastes like kerosene." She gave the apple half back to the bride's mother who sniffed it and said, "You're right, it really does smell like kerosene, maybe it's from the knife."

"So how'd you eat it, Mr. Abd al-Reheem?" asked the bride's uncle.

Abd al-Reheem smiled and said, "I thought that's how apples are supposed to taste," and they all laughed.

As he was leaving, Afkar said to him, "Did you have to let them all know you've never tasted apples before?"

"I was kidding!" he said.

Next day, he dropped in at Nargis and Bahey's, sat on the couch, and said, "Oh, by the way, I divorced Afkar."

"Oh my God!" cried Nargis.

"I sure did," he smiled.

One morning in the large courtyard of the Postal Service building, short, stocky-framed Dos Pasha stood with his left hand in his blue blazer and his right holding a thick cigar. A few steps away stood a British general with several other officers in their military uniforms. Stacked in the corners of the large courtyard were piles of stamped packages and incoming letters for the Allies.

The group's eyes were fixed on the large, steel freight elevator, stuck between the ground and first floors, waiting for the firemen. They arrived with their shiny brass helmets and got on top of it and got it to work. The general was standing in his long shorts and puttees, his hands knotted behind his back, while Dos Pasha, the director of the Postal Service, was puffing on the thick, brown cigar with a noticeable degree of languor and displeasure. Suddenly, the elevator moved up, stopped, then began its descent.

The elevator had two levels with one sliding door. When the servicemen opened it they found remains of food scattered on wrapping paper and a folded blanket on the lower level. On the top level, Abd al-Reheem lay sleeping on his back with his legs crossed and all his underwear off. A small woman with a painted face sat terrified at his feet, and on her disheveled hair was a military cap embossed with the Queen's crown.

The general stood silently and didn't issue any comment, while Dos Pasha looked at the legs of the sleeping watchman and the sitting woman and fingered the crimson kerchief in the top pocket of his blazer. He broke the silence by whispering to one of his assistants who barked at the woman. She half stood and fumbled for her shoes and handbag between Abd al-Reheem's naked legs, then dangled her legs and jumped down, followed by an empty beer bottle which rolled down on the wooden floor and stopped without breaking.

The woman wanted to leave, but one of the officers snatched the cap from her tousled hair, which made her scream and stir the sleeping Abd al-Reheem, who turned on his side and folded his arm under his head, his bare ass facing them. Snoring filled the upper level of the elevator. The officer went up and saluted the general, extending him the folded cap. The general didn't comment or take the cap, but gave Dos Pasha a sidelong glance and left the place, which was soon empty of the officers, who had been transported by three open jeeps left parked by the fire truck. Dos Pasha gestured to the woman to leave, so she ran off, holding her shoes in one hand and the handbag in another, disappearing down a nearby street.

After various attempts to rouse him, Abd al-Reheem's sleep was finally broken and he stretched out on his back, then got on his side again and prepared to fold his arm under his head but stopped and raised his upper body. He looked at them with reddened eyes and appeared to take in the situation. With great effort, he put on his clothes while sitting up under the low steel roof, but he refused to get down. He stayed in place until shortly before noon, when his employment was terminated by administrative order. Then he got off the elevator and left the Postal Service altogether, after looking for al-Bahey Uthman but not finding him. Bahey had been watching along with the others, all the while hiding behind the tall piles of packages, and he had seen everything.

Abd al-Reheem got on the tram and got off on Nile Street, and when he got to Fadlallah Uthman he informed his sister Nargis that they terminated his employment and that he had to go back to the village. He went up to his room on the roof of the building with Nargis following him, "Why'd they fire you, Abd al-Reheem?"

"I don't know."

Then she followed him down: "What train will you take, Abd al-Reheem?"

"The three o'clock."

She followed him down the street and called after him, "Say hello to mother, and Uncle Abd al-Aziz, and don't forget Grandmother Aziza, boy!"

Abd al-Reheem got off the train and made his way to the village entrance carrying his wooden suitcase. He passed by the wheat granary and heard the intermittent whistle of the flour mill, and went into the house. Grandmother Aziza hurried up with her small, bent frame and called out, "Abd al-Reheem's here, Hanem!"

Hanem came running, "Apple of my eye, did you come alone?"

"Yes."

"How's your sister?"

"Fine."

"And her kids?"

"They're good."

Uncle Abd al-Aziz Abu Shanab sat on the wide floor mat between the courtyard and the stable. "Why are you back?" he asked.

"I took a few days off."

The uncle persisted. "Days off?"

"Yes."

"But you just started," he said as he got up, showing the long underwear that revealed his bowed legs. He spit next to the earthenware water urn, and went into the stable.

Abd al-Reheem went into the darkened courtyard and climbed the big stone bench built into the side of the house. He took off the yellow Postal Service uniform and threw it on the top of the wide oven next to the door, put on his gallabiya and skullcap, and strode off in the direction of the shops. He went into al-Labboudi's coffee shop, sat with Abd al-Semee', and ordered tea.

When he returned to work after the 1952 Revolution, Abd al-Reheem moved between several regional branches of the Postal Service, sometimes dispensing stamps and forms, sometimes keeping the books or issuing money orders and disbursing pensions. He considered this a real promotion, especially when he compared himself to al-Bahey Uthman who was still roaming around on a motorcycle, gathering mail from the mailboxes all over the streets of Cairo.

In the beginning, the only thing he noticed about Inshiraah was her huge pension, which was nearly three times his monthly salary. When he cracked open the logbook, his eyes would immediately pick out the large sum in the middle of the list of smaller figures filling the page. Then he noticed that she didn't come on crowded days, when widows, orphans, senior citizens, and ailing people filled the post office and spilled out onto the sidewalk overlooking the square. He didn't blame her when he saw the sad crowds waiting patiently from sunrise until the end of the day. Day after day during these times, he noticed that he and his co-workers spoke in whispers while these poor folk uttered not a sound, despite the stifling crowds and pushing. He felt that the world around him was in an endless state of misery.

Inshiraah used to wait a week or more till things quieted down. Every time he wanted to hand in the pension lists or settle the accounts with the cashier and take a break before the next month's accounts or take a few days off and go to the village, he couldn't until quite late in the month. So he found himself concerned about her without knowing her. Abd al-Reheem remembered this and felt certain that what happened between them afterward was meant to be, and he came to really believe in the popular saying that marriage is a matter of destiny.

She would stride into the nearly empty office with her short, slightly heavy frame, wearing a two-piece dress and a light yellow kerchief tied round her neck, a shiny brass pendant lying on her breast, accompanied by a boy and twin girls, each with two braids. She took out her identification and slid it over the counter, leaning with her elbows on the old wooden surface. While he copied down her identification number, he would inhale her strong perfume that seemed to aim directly for his nose, then he'd turn over the papers to her and point to where she should sign, and notice that she wore her watch on her right hand and that the features of her large, soft face gave it a very respectable air. She said thank you as she put away the money into her handbag without smiling or counting it. But the thing that disconcerted him was that before she left, she always gave him a look that clearly said, "By the way, I've got you all figured out."

He remembered that their first conversation was about dispensing the pension before the prescribed time period. She wanted it early, she said, and though she was taken care of, thank God, we all have responsibilities, and she added in irritation, "The office is always crowded, even though I live nearby."

"Around here?"

"Above Abbas's coffee shop."

"Oh, right on the water."

"Yes, I see you from my balcony on your way back from work." And she added, in distress, that he could come by with the pension money and call from downstairs or come up for coffee.

When the time came to dispense the pension, Abd al-Reheem took it and made his way to her house. She pressed him to come again and soon their relationship deepened. He would bring sacks of fruit for the sake of the boy and twin girls, and would always be surprised that they had a set bedtime at nine o'clock. They would kiss their mother and say, "Good night, Mama. Good night, Uncle." Eventually, he learned to drop by after their bedtime. He liked the apartment with its expensive furniture, the ostrich-feather duster, the small balcony that looked out onto the Nile, the Western-style bathroom, the stove and boiler, and Inshiraah's robes, the heavy and light ones, and the way she would carefully gather them around her to cover her breasts and her full, slightly wrinkled thighs that showed under her short, red nightgown.

She smoked more than he did, and when she got up to empty the glass ashtray of her lipstick-stained cigarette butts, she let the flaps of her robe stay wide open. When he asked her once about her late husband, she leaned on him and burst into tears. He held her close to his chest and patted her soft back and said he didn't mean to hurt her, and she whispered, "Let's not talk about the past, Abd al-Reheem."

He wanted to take her clothes off but she refused. "Please, for me," he begged.

"Absolutely not."

When he offered to marry her, she was deep in thought until she finished her cigarette, then she sighed and accepted. She took the kids to her sister's house in the Rod al-Farag neighborhood. When he slept with her the first time and wanted to get off her, she held him and whispered, "No." He saw the dark crevice of her armpit as she took her fair arm from under the sheets and slipped her fingers under the pillow to take out a small, soft towel. She wrapped it around the base of his member and let him pull out, the towel enveloping and drying him completely.

She took on his whole body, tickling him as he stood and she sat, and she encouraged him to change places and penetrate every part of her, in the middle of the bed and on the edge of the bed, in the kitchen while she was making tea, and on the chairs and the carpet and while she was leaning over the balcony railing smoking and watching the river in the silence of night.

On the seventh day, she refused to stay in her apartment.

"Why?" he asked.

"Because."

"Why can't we just stay here?"

"Why?"

"It's better here."

"Abd al-Reheem, we can't."

She filled a medium suitcase and said, "A few changes of clothes."

"Let's stay away from Nargis."

"Come on, we'll stay a little there and a little here."

Nargis found out and tried hard to find a solution. Bahey insisted on telling Abd al-Reheem's mother Hanem and his uncle Abd al-Aziz. "If we don't say anything, the whole village will say we're the ones who married him off to a divorced woman."

When news reached the village, Uncle Abd al-Aziz snickered and with his crossed eye looked at his sister Hanem with utter disgust. Hanem insisted on going to Cairo and forcing Abd al-Reheem to get divorced, and giving him a beating with her shoe for his awful deed. She sent a letter to Bahey delegating him to deal with the matter and end it as he saw fit. Bahey read the letter as he sat on the couch and said, "Hrmph." Even though Nargis didn't come near his house, Abd al-Reheem would still come by every day, even if only to peek his head through the front door, and when Nargis brought it up he'd chuckle as usual. If a couple of days went by and he didn't come, she would send her son Abdalla to find out what Abd al-Reheem was up to.

Inshiraah went on wearing her short satin nighties underneath her robes, which she folded on the back of the chair, and she also went on tightening her robe around her body to cover her breasts and full, slightly wrinkled thighs as she sat facing him smoking a cigarette. She made up the small room for the boy and two girls and fetched them from her sister's. On their day off, she'd take them to her old apartment so they could bathe with hot water and change clothes and play with their toys, while she would wax her face and body, dye her hair, bathe and rub her heels well with the pumice stone, returning at the end of the day. When Abd al-Reheem ran into her in the long hallway or a corner of the dark courtyard or outside the bathroom, he was fear stricken; she looked like a completely different woman. When he passed behind her as she was sitting down, he noticed the tiny hairs on the back of her neck, white and undyed. She snored softly as she slept, and kept medication pills with her cigarettes and lighter in her robe pocket. His visits to Nargis lasted longer into the night, and Nargis wouldn't stop talking about it.

"But she smokes," Nargis said.

Abd al-Reheem chuckled, "Doesn't cost me anything, she has a huge pension."

Bahey turned. "What?! you mean she hasn't told Pensions about the marriage?"

Abd al-Reheem was silent.

"She should have informed them the day after the marriage."

Nargis asked, "Oh my God, is this true?"

Abd al-Reheem clarified, "Yes, so they could cut it off."

"So you know?"

"It totally slipped my mind."

Bahey commented, "You could go to jail for this."

"Why, what's it got to do with me?"

"What's it got to do with you?! Boy, you're her husband!"

Bahey clarified, "If only he was just her husband—he's also the one who disburses the pension." He smiled sorrowfully. "When the government finds out, they'll say the boss was a thief."

Nargis said, "What are you going to do, Abd al-Reheem?"

"Oh, don't worry. I'll tell her when I see her."

"Tell her? Oh shut up, you idiot," said Nargis.

He returned home late that night and addressed Inshiraah as he hammered a nail into the wall outside the bedroom, saying that a friend of his named Mr. Osama alerted him that she had to inform Pensions about the marriage. Inshiraah didn't answer him until he finished hammering and came into the bedroom.

"Is this friend of yours from the coffee shop or work?"

"From work."

"Why didn't you say anything when you came back from work, then?"

"It totally slipped my mind."

Inshiraah said she could never let go of the pension, and Abd al-Reheem bent down to put the hammer under the bed, straightened up, then sat facing her. She gathered the robe around her bare legs, lit a cigarette, and said, "Absolutely not, it's for the kids. How do you think I can raise them?" She thought a little, then said, "We made a mistake, Abd al-Reheem, and we have to make amends."

"How?"

"We should get divorced."

"Normal people make amends by getting married, and we get divorced?"

She accompanied him to the marriage registrar and then returned to her apartment.

With the passing of time, her apartment became more closed off. He would go back and forth on the riverbank, his eyes on the shuttered window and closed balcony door. Sometimes he noticed what appeared to be another man's shadow moving behind the shutters, and he would lie in wait for him. He was in a state of constant agitation as he remembered the details of what went on between them, and spurned food and no longer slept. He thought about the time of his engagement to Afkar and how it was never like this, not even the time when he was in love with Basima a la Mode, even though she was ten times more beautiful, and young. When he remembered Basima, he was full of hatred for Inshiraah, but he wanted to see her one more time, at any price.

She faced him silently at the door, then told him the kids were sleeping. He begged to be let in, told her that he had important things to say, then sat facing her, gathering his freshly ironed gallabiya in his lap. "Tell me the truth," he said. She turned toward him, and he continued, "Did I do anything to upset you?"

"It's not about that," she said and tears rolled down her cheeks. He put his hand on her knee, wanting her badly.

"Please, Abd al-Reheem."

"I can't leave you while you're crying."

"Come on now."

"Please, for me?"

"Are you crazy?"

He had gone down on his knees and placed his hands on her thighs, trapping her with his stomach in the big chair. "I can't live without you," he said.

He stuffed his hand under her nightgown and forced her thighs apart, and she resisted him with all her strength and panted, "The kids!" But Abd al-Reheem locked his lips on hers and completely paralyzed her. He carried her into the bedroom and flung her on the bed, grabbing her by the hair with one hand and taking his clothes off with the other until he took complete control of her. He thrust hard and noticed her panting and how she kept turning her head and pulling out the hairs that were getting stuck in her mouth. When he finished, he stayed inside her until he was completely relaxed, then got up.

He put on his long underwear and stood up to straighten his gallabiya. He saw her as she sat slumped on the bed, her fair, wrinkled thighs set apart, the tears messing her eyeliner, leaving two ink-colored lines on the face powder caked over her sagging cheeks. She dried her dull eyes with the raised hem of her nightgown, while the robe hung on her shoulders and spread out behind her on the wet pillow.

In the evening, Bahey shaved one more time and put on his suit and tie, Nargis and the kids got dressed, and they all went to the wedding taking place in the village square that lay at the foot of the largest pyramid. There was a huge crowd, men, women, and children everywhere, and ululations, drums, traditional woodwind instruments, stick-dancing, and dancing horses. It was all a big festival. Bahey smiled and Nargis said, "You've really done it this time, Abd al-Reheem."

Soad was Mr. Osama's sister. Mr. Osama worked with Abd al-Reheem at the Postal Service. Nargis noticed that Soad seemed thinner than when she first saw her when she came with Abd al-Reheem to ask for her hand. Uncle Abd al-Aziz had disappeared from the village and Abd al-Reheem's mother Hanem had refused to leave her sick mother Aziza to attend the wedding. Abd al-Reheem had stopped wearing the gallabiya out of the house now and took to wearing a shirt and trousers. He realized that his grandmother's illness (and she was never sick) meant that she was about to die. And if she did die, then his marriage would have to be delayed for at least a year, so he preferred to get it over with, especially since the bride's father, Mr. Murtagi, promised not to impose any financial burdens on him.

Soad's face was beautiful in its white and red makeup, as she sat on the dais in her wedding dress watching the dancing and tapping her feet, her mouth constantly open. Abd al-Reheem sat next to her in suit and tie, clearing his lap of all the cigarette ash and pushing away the kids who kept standing behind his seat and leaning on his head and shoulders. At the end of the evening, when they got ready to get into the van rented for the occasion, Nargis, Abd al-Reheem, and Soad sat in the middle seat and Bahey sat up front next to the driver, while Abdalla and his siblings took the back seat. Mr. Murtagi brought over his daughter's belongings, tied up in a big sheet, and secured it to the top of the van. He stood before them with his long moustache and turbaned head, the whole family behind him. Nargis noticed his mud-colored toes sticking out of his green plastic slippers, as he held onto the hem of his gallabiya, revealing his skinny legs. A loud voice called out, "Goodbye now. Go ahead, Abd al-Fattah." The van turned to leave the clearing in the shadow of the pyramid, followed by a huge procession of children, while Abd al-Fattah, the driver, constantly tooted the horn.

The fact of the matter was that thin Soad was reticent, and she would walk around in her housedress with her head held high, which gave her a supercilious air that made Nargis apprehensive and unsure how to deal with her. Even though when she did talk it was normal, Nargis listened to her and stayed quiet because she found her style not conducive to bantering. Abd al-Reheem would bring her over to spend the evening with them, and she would sit cross-legged on the edge of the sofa and listen to them quietly. A look of surprise filled her eyes as she looked at Abdalla, who was a young man now, and when Abd al-Reheem talked about her father being the first person to set up shop in the pyramids plateau "before Soad was born," she would comment, "A dry measure of crushed beans cost a piaster back then," and then fall silent.

This kind of talk was what Nargis meant and talked about with Bahey. A faint smile would appear on Bahey's lips as he fingered his worry beads and thought to himself, "Why crushed beans in particular?"

Each evening, Abd al-Reheem talked about the treasure buried in the ancient Egyptian tomb over which Murtagi had built his house. Nargis had seen this house on the day of the engagement party. It was a one-story house and she found its rooms rather large, most of them opening onto each other, with untiled dirt floors. The bathroom was large and there they kept chickens, white geese, and a red billy goat. The old-fashioned bathroom's hole in the ground was in the middle of the floor and Nargis was too embarrassed to hike up her clothes and relieve herself in front of all these creatures.

Abd al-Reheem said to her, "That's what we've been saying all along." He went on to explain to her how Mr. Murtagi placed the hole in the ground right above the well that connected to the tomb vault so that nobody could discover it. "All the houses are like that." And he smiled at her and asked if she remembered the man who wore the cloak.

"What man?"

"At the wedding."

"Your and Soad's wedding?"

"Yes."

"How could I remember him, it's been a year!"

"The fat man?" Bahey asked.

"No, the bald one."

"Bald?"

"Yes, you know, the guy who was standing next to Mr. Murtagi all the time."

And Soad would comment, "Feryal's father."

Bahey looked at her and then back to Abd al-Reheem. "What about him?"

"That guy found a piece of marble this big in the tomb underneath his house," and he held his arms wide apart. "And arranged around it was a golden chicken with seven chicks."

"Oh my God!"

Abd al-Reheem laughed, "Yes, what'd you think?"

"And what about Mr. Murtagi?"

Abd al-Reheem sighed, saying that they were still trying because the well to their tomb is very deep. "Every time they go down the bulb goes out."

"Before the horse died," Soad commented.

"Horse?"

"Yes, some people find a chicken and eggs instead of the chicks."

Nargis turned to her and asked, "Also gold?"

Soad pulled the hem of her gallabiya down to her toes and

said, "But they have to have ropes." This made Nargis even more angry toward her.

Soad's mother died when she was young and her older sister Afaf had raised her and her other siblings. They grew up at the foot of the pyramids and made their living off of the foreign tourists and spoke their languages. Back then, Murtagi owned a horse decorated with colorful silk flowers that they rented to tourists by the hour. But the horse died, and Murtagi mourned it and took people's condolences as if it was a person. As for the kids, they spread out all over: two boys in Italy and one who they sometimes heard was in Libya and other times in Iraq. Osama was the only one who finished elementary school and got a job at the Postal Service. He spent most days traveling on trains, transporting sacks of mail.

Afaf was a widow with small children who lived with her father, who now had ailing feet. Every day, they carried him outside and leaned his back on the small wall facing the large pyramid, his wrist leaning on the horse's saddle, which he had refused to part with. The pyramid took up three quarters of the world in front of him, and the remaining quarter had a reasonable amount of sky and he could see the low, slanted houses, as well as the sacks of lentils, green beans, and crushed beans stacked at the front of his shop. Murtagi felt that he'd completed his life's work by marrying off his youngest daughter to Abd al-Reheem.

He would sit with his sick feet stretched out before him, smoking, eating, and yelling at the kids, who paid no attention to him seeing as how he couldn't stand up on his own. He spent the day like this until he fell asleep, moustache drooping, his head on his chest or shoulder, and then they carried him into the house. While asleep he was heavy as a corpse and Afaf could not carry him into the house without help, and so many times she had to cover him up and leave him outside until the next morning, when he would wake up and resume his perch without saying a word or getting angry.

Soad went to her father's house often; Abd al-Reheem would come back from work to an empty house and know she was there. She stayed for a few days, caring for her sister Afaf's kids. Afaf juggled the kids, Murtagi, and the shop and her health was gone completely. Soad never returned of her own accord, Abd al-Reheem always had to go and fetch her. Every time, she brought with her some beans, rice, lentils, or eggs, and one or two of her nephews. Nargis dropped by and saw that everything was fine but that Soad hadn't become pregnant yet.

"How's your father, Soad?" Nargis asked.

"Fine, thank God, but he's dying."

A few days later, he died. Soad went to man the shop and Afaf stayed home with the kids, while Mr. Osama disappeared into his work on the postal cars accompanying trains.

Abd al-Reheem got used to visiting Soad there, seeing her barefoot and wearing men's pajama pants under her gallabiya. He'd spent a night or two with them, sleep with Soad wherever possible, and leave. Soad would go to Fadlallah Uthman every week or two, take some of her clothes, and leave. Over time, she took all of her things and stopped going.

4

THE HOUSE, AS Abd al-Reheem and his family called it, was formerly the courtyard of a large, stone building built in the early twentieth century, with a wooden door that Hagg Abbas al-Kebir had forced open during World War II to enable him to get out onto Fadlallah Uthman and to the riverbank during intense air raids. The upper floors occupied by the other tenants had a separate entrance on a back street.

This courtyard had three skylights. Abd al-Reheem had received it completely unfinished save for a large room with one wide window with bars on it on the left of the passageway. At the end of the long passageway were empty rooms connected by straight or angled corridors, and in the middle of one of the rooms was a low toilet.

Over the years, Abd al-Reheem built several fixed and sliding skylights that transformed the place into a rural home known only to its denizens. He left open spaces for the sunlight to enter during winter, and built small north-facing windows, one facing his mother's room and another facing the long corridor across from the entrance, which opened onto Fadlallah Uthman. He also built a ground toilet elevated above the floor by three bricks and covered the walls surrounding it with wood paneling. He would bring old slabs of wood from the market and stock them up for his impulsive projects. He made a chicken coop with a screen door and a small feedsack for a billy goat that he had bought before one of the feast days after his mother had expressed interest in a sacrifice. When Dalal came from the countryside, he made her a kitchen with shelves and a window looking out onto the large, clay water-storage urn. He'd built a holder for the urn out of brick and cement and placed an empty ghee tin underneath it to collect falling water drops.

The walls were studded with long nails from which hung clumps of dried okra, red chilli peppers, onions, and garlic. As Mr. Abdalla ibn Uthman made his way to his missing grandmother's room, he bent down below the clotheslines hung between the nails. There were round straw baskets filled with mint and mulukhiyya leaves left out to dry, and a group of sieves and baskets filled with pieces of bread, flour, and bran. In one corner, there was an upside down, round, earthen dough trough used as a stool, and shelves built into the walls that held large kerosene lamps, nightlights, empty boxes, and packages wrapped in paper and tied with strips of fabric.

Abd al-Reheem had also built a long, low bench in a far corner of the courtyard on which he placed a long cushion for napping, far away from the sound of the radio and the kids playing. When his mother Hanem arrived from the village, she asked for a stove to be put near her small room, which she used until the kids started sitting on it and defecating and urinating on it. From time to time, Abd al-Reheem would mix cement and sand to cover the walls whose mortar was peeling to reveal the rubble beneath, which was put together haphazardly; or he would add another sewer to the ones dug near the walls, which all dovetailed into one main pipeline that flowed into a round drain in the corner of the courtyard.

Mr. Abdalla stopped at his grandmother's room on the right.

It was dark and empty, saturated with the smell of damp bread. Her small bed was made, the rug old and faded, and in the dark corner stood her wooden trousseau with its engraved, rusty copper locks. He knew that his uncle had long ago meant this room to be the kitchen in preparation for his marriage to Afkar, the marriage that was never consummated. Then he got it ready for Inshiraah's three children to sleep in when he was married to her. The room became a kitchen again during his third, short-lived marriage to Soad. The house had changed completely since the arrival of Abd al-Reheem's mother Hanem and his marriage to Dalal, the girl from their home village, who became pregnant a month and a few days after the wedding.

Dalal would leave them to go to sleep. When Abd al-Reheem came home early, she would fix them tea before turning in. No matter what time Abd al-Reheem returned, Hanem would hear his movements as he unfastened the package and put its contents on a plate, calling out to her, "Get up, Ma." She sat with him at the front of the courtyard with Fadlallah Uthman stretched out before them. Every once in a while, she picked up a crumb of the food he always brought: a small bit of feta or Kasseri cheese or a piece of halvah, in addition to a few olives, sometimes black and sometimes green. She spent the evening chewing thimble-sized pieces of bread or cheese, and if she tried to chew an olive with her toothless gums, she swallowed it with the pit by mistake. So she stayed away from olives despite her fondness for them. When he brought a new kind of cheese such as cream cheese, cheddar, or Roquefort he would draw her attention to it until reassured that she noticed the difference in taste. They talked all night about their village or its chief Abd al-Rahman, their land, or Nargis, or anything at all until the peep of dawn rose over Fadlallah Uthman.

When Abd al-Reheem died, Hanem's grandson Mr. Abdalla

ibn al-Bahey Uthman bought her the same kinds of food and gave it to Dalal to arrange in the plate and put in the front of the courtyard, because his grandmother still left her room at night and sat at her usual place. Time would pass and she would laugh and say, "That boy Abd al-Reheem is late," and Dalal, trying to keep an eye on her as sleep overtook her, would reply, "He'll be here soon." Sometimes Hanem would touch her inside pocket to make sure the two ten-pound notes were still there, the money she had put away years ago to finance her funeral: the money for the car that would transport her from Cairo the village; the shroud for her body; the undertaker's fee; the female mourners' fee; the fee for the stentorian-voiced Shaykh Mustafa al-Safti, the well-known Qur'an reciter (who had died thirty-four years ago); and also the dinner that Nargis would prepare for their neighbors from Fadlallah Uthman. Even though this pouch where she kept the money was fastened onto her inner slip with a safety pin, a few years ago Abd al-Reheem managed to unhook the pin and take out the banknotes, replacing them with folded lined notebook paper. Dalal knew because when she did laundry he asked her not to tell his mother about the folded notebook paper in the pouch.

For her part, Dalal wasn't shocked by anything he did after she saw him tie his ailing tooth to a thread attached to a nail in the wall. He lit a cigarette to distract himself and asked her to talk to him about anything. "What do you want me to talk to you about?" she asked him. "You're so stubborn. I told you . . ." he said, and jerked his head back suddenly. At the end of the thread hung his long, dark tooth.

There was no formality at all between them. A few months after their marriage, he started walking around naked and shamelessly uttered curse words in front of her and his mother. During the summer and even the winter months, Dalal went around the house wearing a thin-strapped gown with nothing underneath, and he would startle her and slap her on the behind, cornering her. He mounted her with his heavy body and she moaned at the way he kneaded her breasts. He laughed and trapped her with his thighs, hitting her womb with his member in those intimate, practiced thrusts. She was used to him the way her ears got used to the sound of his farts occasionally resounding in the corners of the house.

"Should I make you some more tea?"

Mr. Abdalla said, "No thanks, I'm leaving soon."

Dalal said that every time the power went out she thought she was back in the village, and that if only Abd al-Reheem (God forgive him and have compassion on him) had listened to her and sold the land, gave Nargis her share and used his share to build a house in place of the large house he sold for nothing, she would have taken the kids and gone to live there on his pension. "But here we are, cut off, no family, no house, no land, no village," she sighed.

Her boy Abdalla had fallen asleep. Mr. Abdalla stood in the middle of the room, his hands in his pockets, contemplating the hung photograph. "Where is this land, exactly?"

"In the village, Mr. Abdalla."

"You mean all the way inside the village?"

Dalal explained that there were no fields inside the village, all the fields bordered the village center. When you go out of the train station, on the other side of the tracks, as far as the eye could see, were the fields and farmland.

"Who's there now?"

"What do you mean?"

"Who's renting it?"

Dalal said, "Abd al-Rahman, the village chief, swallowed it up and registered it in his name along with some other fields, then he rented it out to someone who died a while ago and his children died too." She added, "God only knows if his children's children are farming it these days or if they've rented it out to someone else. We're hoping you can find this out."

Mr. Abdalla heard these words and quickly realized that he was embarking on a completely new experience. His intuition convinced him that he wouldn't reach any concrete solution to this matter, but of course he would do his duty as befits his status as the family elder now. He wondered whether he should prepare them psychologically for the failure of this land issue they put so much store by or keep silent and wait until the time comes. Just then, the power suddenly came back on and Salama called out from the doorway, "The light arrives with the new arrivals," and he sat down.

When Dalal came in with the tea, he spread his arms out on the armrests and asked if there was any news. When no one said anything, he said he had asked everyone he saw about his missing grandmother. "Sitting around like this is useless," said Salama.

Mr. Abdalla was annoyed at this way of talking and his face showed signs of disapproval. At this moment, he thought his brother was well-meaning but ultimately he was an ass, and the old thing between them which happened for completely objective reasons did not at all justify Salama placing himself as equal to Mr. Abdalla, especially from an intellectual vantage point.

True, the feelings of tension and unease with all those Mr. Abdalla met after his release were noticeable, but it was mutual. For years, he saw in their eyes what he did not understand, and he still did not know how they interpreted his words and to what degree he could unwind with this or that person. His father had died in his long absence, and his mother greeted him with open arms, running out barefoot onto Fadlallah Uthman. It was he who cried. As for her, Nargis, she went back to her old self, overcoming grief, sickness, and fatigue. She made him breakfast and woke him up, took him his tea, told him what happened on Fadlallah Uthman. "Abdalla, son, you won't believe what happened to your uncle Ahmed al-Rashidi." He followed her stories with quizzical, smiling, hopeful eyes. She was resuming topics he did not know nor remember.

Mr. Abdalla spent the night at Leila's and in the morning returned to Fadlallah Uthman. He went up the few steps and knocked on the glass part of the door. Nargis called out, "Who is it?"

"It's me, Ma."

"Oh, Abdalla," and she opened the door. He was taken aback by the living room full of smoke, and looked at his mother running into the kitchen and panting, "Close the door behind you."

She was sitting by the toilet with papers ablaze in front of her, soot everywhere, an open leather bag next to her right knee, and the broom prone nearby. He recognized the bag and the papers. "What're you doing, Ma? How'd these papers get here?"

"Be patient, Abdalla." She took some papers and set them on fire, then turned on the tap and let the water run over the burning papers as she swept it all away. She zipped up the empty bag and got up, leaning on her knees. "It was full to the brim," she said. She turned to him and added, "Open the window."

Morning sunlight poured in, lighting the clouds of smoke and the right arm of the couch. Nargis took a towel and started swinging it around, airing out the room, then sat in her favorite place where the two sofas met and dried her perspiring face with the hem of her outer gallabiya while gathering her inner gallabiya around her.

She coughed and said, "You'll never believe what happened."

"What?"

"The government people."

"Government?"

"They went around asking for your friend Hamama and his wife."

"Where'd they ask?"

"In the building they used to live in." She pointed to the empty leather bag and said, "If I'd known you were coming now I would have left it, but I was scared they'd search like last time."

"Did Hamama bring it here?"

"No, Salama did."

"Salama my brother?"

"He brought it over as soon as your father left." She said the landlord where Hamama and his wife lived told the government that it was Salama who brought them to live there. "You should've seen him when he found out the government people asked about him too."

"Where is he now?"

"Hiding out at his mother-in-law's."

"I have to see him."

"He'll be here soon. Have you had breakfast yet?"

Mr. Abdalla went out to Fadlallah Uthman. Salama was leaning against the wall underneath his mother-in-law's low window. He pointed to him and he approached hurriedly, then walked normally and climbed the few steps after Abdalla, saying, "Can you believe what's happened?"

When they sat in the outer room, he stretched his arms on the armrests, and when his eyes met his brother's, he was on the verge of tears. His face was youthful and radiant then.

Abdalla took out his cigarettes but Salama declined. Nargis came out with a clean bowl and asked Salama to go out and get the morning fuul so that he and his brother could have breakfast. "Yes, Ma," he said as he took the plate and put it next to him without getting up.

Abdalla said, "First of all, I want to know all about the bag. Who'd you get it from, and why'd you take it?"

"I didn't take it," Salama said. "We left it for safekeeping with Hamama's wife, Samia."

"When?"

"Before they moved out."

"Why didn't you tell me?"

"I just found out yesterday, by accident. When the government asked about Hamama and his wife, the landlord told them they'd moved out, and that I would know their new address because I was the one who brought them, and then the government came knocking on my door. But I was here at the time."

"So how'd you know that they came by?"

"When I returned in the evening the neighbors told me."

"What exactly did they tell you?"

"Hand me a cigarette. They told me that furniture salesmen from Damietta asked about Hamama and his wife because they owed late installments. Saad the mechanic told me they came in a government car and parked it behind the mosque. Of course I understood. When I talked to Samia, she remembered the bag and took it out from under the bed." He blew smoke and continued, "Furniture, my foot! They were sleeping on the bare floor, man."

Nargis called out from the living room. "Get up, Salama, and go get the fuul and have breakfast first."

He said, "Yes, Ma," but he didn't move.

Abdalla sat smoking and thinking. "It's simple," he said. "If anyone asks you about them, you say you ran into them by accident and they were looking for an apartment in the area. You told them about the apartment next to you. Apart from this, you don't know anything about them."

Salama asked, "Who would be asking this?"

Abdalla said, "Anybody who might ask you."

"Where'd they see me to ask me?"

"At your house, for instance."

"And why'd I go there?"

"So where are you going to go then?"

"Anywhere."

"You're not thinking straight."

"You want me to go there and wait for them?"

"Of course. They should see you at home, living your regular life and you should deal with them as if they really are furniture dealers from Damietta. If you leave your house, it would look suspicious, as if you're running away."

Salama sat thinking. Nargis's voice filtered in from the outside telling him to listen to his brother and to go get the beans because she'd started making tea.

Just then they heard knocking on the door. Salama shot up, while Abdalla looked at the open window. Nargis called out, "Who is it?"

"It's me, Samia's father."

Salama sat back down while Nargis opened the door. Hagg Farid came in, holding his dirty hands away from his gallabiya. "What's going on, Salama?"

"Nothing," said Salama.

"Oh Lord." He saw Abdalla out of the corner of his eye, and said, "What've you got to do with these things?"

He sighed, "I'll be going now."

"Tea, Hagg Farid," called Nargis. Hagg Farid said he had taken apart the water pump and left it in the courtyard. "For two days we haven't been able to get a drink of water. It's disgusting. I've got to go, goodbye."

Abdalla said, "What's happening now is dangerous. You tell your wife, she tells her father, he goes around telling everyone he sees. You're supposed to not know anything except that these people are simply furniture dealers from Damietta." He asked Salama to tell Samia and Hagg Farid right away not to talk about this at all. He pointed out that if the government found out that Hamama and his wife knew him and that Salama is his brother, everyone would go to hell.

For a minute, Salama was preoccupied with what he had noticed when Hagg Farid knocked on the door. Later, when Nargis had him alone and asked him to do everything his brother said, he turned to her as he held the door and said, "By the way, Ma, when Hagg Farid knocked, Abdalla wanted to jump out the window."

It was clear in his mind: if the government cornered him and asked him, he'd say that Hamama and his wife are his brother's friends, and that it was Abdalla himself who asked him to find them a place near him. Aside from this, he knew nothing about them. Samia expressed surprise and he said, "Come on, don't you know the saying 'When the flood comes in, throw your kid beneath you'?"

The problem was the strange state that betook him, that made him go to his mother's house instead of to the printing house, the state of constant diarrhea that seized him during the day, making him run like he'd never run before, and at night, pushing him to the riverbank or any dark corner. He would undo his belt and squat, kicking up dust, writhing in pain and shame, with no help. Salama was struggling on more than one front.

That day, he climbed the steps two at a time, as was his wont the last few days. Panting, he took off his shoes and pants in the small apartment's living room, barely missing the little boy on the floor playing with the empty Turkish coffee pot. He raced into the bathroom as Samia got up from behind her sewing machine, put away his shoes and hung up his pants. She put out the low, round eating table and came back with a plate of mulukhiyya soup and boiled chicken thighs. As he sat down and fed the boy a piece of chicken, she asked him, "Will you have a siesta?"

"Hopefully."

"I wanted you to fix the hem of Farida's gallabiya and fasten on the buttons."

"When I wake up."

He washed his hands and lit a cigarette, and raced once again to the bathroom. During his ordeal, he heard distant voices and unintelligible words, then a knock on the bathroom door and Samia peered in, her face lemon-yellow with fright. "They're here, Salama, they're here," she whispered. He contemplated her terrified face as he sat holding his clothes around him, cigarette in hand, and found himself saying, "Don't worry about a thing." He started washing up even though he hadn't done anything yet. On his way out, he bumped into Samia as she was putting away the low eating table and said angrily, "Watch out." Then he turned to them and said, "Welcome, sit down."

There were three of them. They came into the room, looking around at everything. Salama stood at the entrance, smiling. "Well, coffee or tea?"

"No, thank you," said the youngest, while another one was looking at a photograph of the Zamalek soccer team with the

Egypt Cup in front of them. Salama put his head back out of the room and brought it close to Samia's, who was standing immediately behind the door. They looked at each other and she whispered, "It's them, right?" He didn't answer. He called out as if she was in the kitchen, "The tea, Mrs. Salama." He turned back to them and offered cigarettes, but they declined.

"We asked about you a few days ago."

"I know, they told me." He said the neighbors had told him salesmen from Damietta asked about Hamama and that he was very upset that he wasn't there, adding that his mother was very sick and that he had to go see her daily.

The young one said they wanted to see Hamama and his wife and Salama said, "I wish you could," and he told them that it was by chance that he found out they had moved out.

"We know your relationship with them, your neighbors told us," the young one said.

Salama's smile faded. He said, "If I knew where they were, why would I deny it? My relationship with them began the day I was coming back from work on my bike, back when I had a bike, that is," he laughed nervously. He went on, "It was sunset during Ramadan, the time for breaking the fast and everything was quiet. I got off my bike and was about to go in when a man asked me about nearby housing. It just so happened that the plumber Rizq had an empty room, so I pointed out the house to them. Since then, I've seen the man only once or twice as he was coming to and from his house." He called out, "An ashtray, Mrs. Salama."

In the living room, one of them was studying the family photos put underneath the cracked glass top of the dresser. He looked at them one by one and when he finished, he asked, "How much do you rent this apartment for?"

"Eight pounds a month. It's rent controlled."

The other one made for the bedroom and opened its door. "Same size as the other?"

"A little smaller."

He went into the kitchen, and on his way back peered into the bathroom. Salama said, "But I pay five pounds every week for drainage. There's no sewage system."

"Salama, this piece of paper has our phone number on it. If you find out anything about them, call us right away." And they descended the narrow stairs.

He remained standing until he guessed they would be in the courtyard and then said, "Goodbye." He sat on the couch, leaving the apartment door open. He looked at Samia and asked her to bring over the gallabiya whose hem needed fixing.

When he next went to Fadlallah Uthman and saw Mr. Abdalla, they talked about all kinds of things and then he told him, in passing, that he had met the government, and he recounted the incident in precise detail, sometimes stopping to have a drink or go to the bathroom. Mr. Abdalla listened and then informed him that they'd arrested Hamama. Salama was speechless. He kept silent, obviously hesitating, feeling that there was more. The signs of impending diarrhea showed on his face. "How'd they arrest him?" he asked.

Abdalla said that the state security officers who visited Salama yesterday got hold of the mover who had moved the mattresses, books, and pillows and he told them the new address.

"What about his wife?" whispered Salama.

"She's on the run."

The next day, Abdalla himself was arrested.

While they were going out, Dalal asked Mr. Abdalla to let her know when he got back from the village. "Are you leaving tomorrow?" asked Salama.

"God willing," replied Abdalla.

"Don't forget about the matter of the land."

They were walking down Fadlallah Uthman, and Abdalla noticed that it had gotten smaller or narrower than it used to be, and he was full of wonder at its pavement that kept rising and the entrances to the doors on either side that kept falling. He thought of his boyhood, when the owners of the houses were rebuilding them and made the entrances three steps above street level, thinking that with time it would level with the street. But the street kept rising and the entrances to the houses kept falling. He could always tell the age of a building by how much lower it was than the others. Now he felt pleased that he saw no one he knew. Youth of another generation were standing on the street corners; Salama greeted them as he walked beside him, standing straight and cocky. For his part, Abdalla thought this was silly and contrived. Out of the corner of his eye, he saw Dr. Rifaat's car parked under the open window of the doctor's office.

The last time he had been to Fadlallah Uthman, he saw Sharbaat, who as a young girl long ago used to pursue him with her bold eyes, and played with him on the riverbank in her two long braids. Then she grew up and disappeared like all the other kids. He spotted her, a big pile of flesh sitting cross legged and barefoot at the entrance to one of the houses, and he didn't recognize her. He heard her saying in singsong the famous wartime tune, "How long it's been, my shield." He turned around and recognized her eyes, and her beautiful old smile. Her face lit up when she realized he knew her, and she called out in a loud voice, "Won't you come in?"

"No, thank you," he whispered, feeling something akin to shame.

He thought that this must be the house she used to sit outside, but he wasn't sure. They passed by their old house and its shuttered window above Muhammad al-Rashidi's car, its tires flat and eaten up by dust. How strange. They were sitting behind that very shuttered window in front of the German radio their father had bought from Hassan al-Sudani, when bullets rang out and there was a commotion. He heard a voice saying, "Yes, that's him!" There were lots of loud voices, then Abd al-Nasser's voice rose above them all, "Oh citizens, men, stay put. If Abd al-Nasser dies, then all of you are Gamal Abd al-Nasser!" It was the 1954 assassination attempt in Alexandria. That night, police rounded up members of the Muslim Brothers and searched for weapons in the neighborhood, and in the morning their living room was filled with Muhammad al-Rashidi and his father Hagg Ahmad al-Rashidi and Hagg Mahmoud the coal dealer and his uncle Abd al-Reheem and others, while his father stood holding the newspaper with the defendant's picture. Suddenly he yelled, "Oh my God, it's Mahmoud the handyman!"

He climbed up on the sofa and looked at the picture, but he didn't recognize the man in it. On the way to school each morning, he saw the handyman sitting in his shirt and pants behind a small, corrugated iron table, dark and a little plump, his side to the road as he recited the Qur'an, moving slowly to and fro with a kerchief tied round his head. He thought that the face of the man in the picture was bigger and darker. He ran with the other kids towards the shop, which had a corrugated iron shutter serving as its door and a big lock securing it to the ground. For years it stayed that way until the successive renters came along. Once he saw that it turned into a barbershop. Another time he saw it filled with empty paper cement sacks, with one man cutting them up while another turned them into smaller paper sacks. Now, under a neon light, a young clerk stood fiddling with the small tape recorder, behind a glass table holding jars of sweets and packages of potato chips, colored balloons hanging from the ceiling.

At the intersection, he said goodbye to his brother Salama, noticing the schoolbag store and how its entrance had fallen so that he could see the shoulders of the old man sitting below ground level behind the table with the sewing machine, the naked bulb hanging from the ceiling nearly grazing his bald head. As he made his way to Nile Street, he heard Salama's voice from far away. "Don't forget about the matter of the land."

He sat on the riverbank. The river was still, the street lights reflected on its surface appeared cloudy and faded. Abdalla ibn Uthman thought the water was asleep. The land? This land that his brother is dreaming of—where? How? Originally, it belonged to their great-grandmother Aziza. When she died, her daughter Hanem (their grandmother) inherited a third, and two thirds went to her son Abd al-Aziz, their grandmother's brother. Abd al-Aziz farmed it himself until he died, then the village chief Abd al-Rahman rented it to one of his acquaintances. Abd al-Aziz's children had a right to two-thirds of the rent, and Hanem a third. But Hanem died. So the third goes to Hanem's children: Nargis and Abd al-Reheem. A third to Nargis, two-thirds to Abd al-Reheem. Nargis died, so Abdalla and his siblings should inherit her share. And Abd al-Reheem died, so Dalal and her kids should inherit his share. Dalal told him that the village chief Abd al-Rahman had died and so had the old tenant and his children, but no one knows where the land is or who is living on it now.

A long story with no beginning or end. True, each one who's alive has a right to the land, even if only a square foot, but where, and how? And when he goes to the village, who should he look for? He walked off, thinking.

Long ago, they used to greet them at the train station, bending over him and ruffling his hair. They'd take the suitcases from his father and go to the house, where his grandmother Hanem and her mother Aziza stood at the corner of the large gateway. He knew he would get off the train, cross the highway and make his way to the entrance of the village, with the wheat granary on the right and the windmill on the left, whose whistle would echo in his ear night and day for the entire summer vacation. After walking for a bit he'd find the road forking in two, one stretching in the direction of where he and Salem would go to play by the waterwheel, the large sycamore tree, and the palm tree they planted the day his father was born. "Boy, this palm tree was planted the day I was born," his father would say as he grasped his palm and stood under it. "It's called Bahey's palm tree."

He recalled Sidi Ali al-Shimbabi whom Nargis remembered all her life. And Rashed the mechanic who always returned on the last train and walked home in the dark, drunk; when it was election time he'd slur, "Down with God!" frightening village residents. Then he grew a beard and wore a gallabiya and became one of God's devout followers.

Once, he ate some of the fruit of the sycamore tree floating in the pond, and at night he threw up and they woke up Salem, who reassured them that nothing would happen.

The other road led to shops and a big sieve on the left side of the road, a barn, and the lake, and the house of his grandmother and her mother. His great-uncle Abd al-Aziz made him a rope swing and hung it from the roof of their house.

Once, he ate a brown aubergine he'd picked himself from a short, green tree. Once, he went into a field and saw boys sitting in a semicircle, chewing the virility plant and rubbing their erect, naked members. Salem told him that they were testing to see whether they'd become men yet. Once, some kids were chasing the sparrows that nested in the ceiling of the large house. They caught them with upside down hats and gave him one, but it flew off right away. Once, his uncle Abd al-Reheem took him for a night out with some young men on a bench by the big lake. They looked up in silence at a large, mud brick mansion with a row of long, dark windows. Suddenly, a faint orange light shone from one of the windows, the light of a portable lamp. They saw a face with long hair, then the light went out. Someone whispered, "Aida."

When he was little, kids his age would set their bird traps by the riverbank and cover them up with delicate layers of dust or shrubs, only the tiny worms showing through, or the grains of wheat or rice they used to bait these wire traps. As he stood watching, he'd see a trap clamp down, throwing up a stream of dust or hay as it held onto one of the small sparrows after it had been flying between the branches of the leaning trees and the sloping riverbank. He got himself a trap but he never succeeded in catching a sparrow like the other kids, who used to brag about catching more than one sparrow a day. They tied them up with thin string and let them swing, injured, and then they'd fall. The kids held the ends of the string and laughed. He tried his luck all along the riverbank; he moved his trap to different places, put out wheat and rice and tiny worms, but failure was always his due. Nargis knew, which intensified his feelings of weakness and shame toward his peers, and pain.

Once, he went to buy something. On his way back, he saw a sparrow limping, leaning on the wall. He scooped him up and put him in his gallabiya pocket, climbing the steps. He gave his mother what she'd asked for, careful to appear normal, then took his trap from under the side table and told her he was going to catch a sparrow. He went out as if going to the river-bank, then surreptitiously made his way up to the roof. He wanted to put it in the trap, wait a while, and then go back to his mother carrying the sparrow as if he'd just caught it. He got up on the big rock on the roof, took the sparrow out of his pocket, and opened the trap. He tried to gently clamp it down on the sparrow's neck, but it twittered with pain. He tried its legs, wings, but the sparrow kept aching.

His heart wasn't in it, so he stopped to think about this prob-lem. Suddenly, the sparrow threw him a sharp stare and scratched him with its thin, sharp claws. It scuffed him and jumped. He leaned over to see it, following its descent with light outstretched wings, coming to rest on the lower roof of the next building. After a while, it tried again, but kept descending until it was trapped by the walls of the houses in the narrow side alley. It was about to fall in the circle of kids, who were jump-ing up to try and catch it, while it grasped the rough rocks in flight. It turned toward them, flapping its wings from one wall to the next until worn down by fatigue, and at that minute he realized that the sparrow was doomed. But the sparrow had learned to fly, and suddenly it hovered above him, circling twice, then dashed past the gates and trees, rose up in the far wide sky, and disappeared.

Slowly he went up the steps, opened the door, and stood in the living room. Through the half-open bedroom door he saw his sleeping wife's feet, and then he went into the children's room. Each was in his metal-framed bed, the older one had drawn up the covers to his neck, the younger one had kicked the sheets down to the foot of the bed. He pulled them up and swaddled him tightly. As he was leaning over the sleeping child, patting his back, Abdalla ibn Uthman felt his father's hand on his shoulder from behind, and he shuddered in the darkness.

5

In the men's ward, Dalal sat on the tiled floor next to the small metal cabinet, which had arranged on it the medicines, the health insurance card, a pitcher, and a glass. When her stomachache felt severe, she stretched her legs out under the bed or played with the yellow hose hanging from the oxygen cylinder. Every now and then, she raised herself up to check on Abd al-Reheem, who had been bedridden for days, his heart weak, and the swelling spreading to his face and feet. If she saw that his head was hanging too low on his chest or that his tongue was sticking out or that his breathing had stopped, she pulled herself up, holding onto the side of the bed for support, and opened the oxygen tube like they showed her. She held the thin hose to his open mouth and nose until he revived and started breathing regularly. Then she'd shut it off and return to her place, busying herself with whatever came to her mind, or re-arranging the items on the cabinet, or going to the bathroom, or asking him, "You want me to squeeze you a lemon, Abd al-Reheem?"

"Sit down."

"What'd you say? I can't hear you."

"Is my sister Nargis here yet?"

"Not yet."

"Did her son Abdalla come?"

"Not yet. You need something?"

"I want a cigarette." He leaned over and whispered, "That guy over there, with the fez, go get a cigarette from him and tell him Abdalla will give him one when he comes."

Dalal looked around and said, "Where is this guy? Everyone's sleeping, Abd al-Reheem, and no one's wearing a fez."

"All right, be quiet."

"Huh?"

"Be quiet."

"Fine, I'll be quiet," and she sat down.

The small ward held four beds with patients suffering from heart disease and renal failure. During the days she stayed with Abd al-Reheem, Dalal figured out the way to the nurses' room, the bathroom, and the street. She opened the cabinet and fussed with the slips of paper in the medicine boxes, smiling to herself, and did not hear Nargis come in panting in her black dress. Nargis sat on the edge of the bed, carrying a sack of oranges.

"How are you feeling today, Abd al-Reheem?"

"Your sister's here, Abduh," said Dalal, still smiling.

"My sister who?"

"Abdalla's mother."

"How are you, Nargis?" asked Abd al-Reheem.

"I'm fine, how are you?"

"I'm fine."

"How are you, Dalal?" asked Nargis.

"Fine, Auntie," she took the sack of oranges from her and stuffed it into the cabinet.

"You want me to peel you one, Abd al-Reheem?"

"One what?"

"Orange."

"No."

Dalal peeled one and started eating it but the stomachache really hurt now and pinched her abdomen. She thought of leaving Abd al-Reheem with Aunt Nargis and going to see a doctor so he could prescribe something, but she remembered that she'd left Fadlallah Uthman hurriedly with Abd al-Reheem to the hospital without putting on her underpants. She put half the orange on the cabinet and stood up, leaning over him. "Abd al-Reheem? Abduh?"

He opened his eyes without raising his head or answering.

"Can you hear me?"

"Yes."

Nargis listened in, but Dalal whispered into Abd al-Reheem's right ear and asked him to give her his underpants. "So that I can wear them when they examine me and then I'll return them to you."

"What?!"

"Give me your underpants so that I can wear them while they check my stomach."

Nargis leaned over, looking from one to the other without hearing what they were saying. "What's going on, kids?" she asked.

Abd al-Reheem's head felt heavy for a spell, then Nargis heard him ask whether this meant that Dalal was standing there without underpants?

Nargis slapped her bosom in shock and said, "Oh my God! What's this you're talking about, Abd al-Reheem?"

"Just till I go to the doctor and back," explained Dalal.

"You bitch!" exclaimed Abd al-Reheem.

Dalal smiled as she turned around, and he was unconscious again. When he came to, he said, "My underpants?"

Nargis put her hand over her toothless mouth and said, "Oh my goodness, what is going on?"

"Come on, Abduh. It's not like I'll eat them," said Dalal.

"Oh Tafida's daughter, you bitch," said Abd al-Reheem.

"Shame on you, Abd al-Reheem," whispered Nargis.

"Be quiet, Nargis," he said.

"All right, but keep your voice down," said Nargis.

"I'm not going to keep my voice down, I have to expose her."

He started gasping for air. Dalal quickly made for the oxygen tube, and Nargis watched her open the spigot and move the hose in front of his mouth and nose. Abd al-Reheem calmed down and let his head fall on Dalal's full bosom. Quietly, Nargis reached for the hose that Dalal had left on the edge of the bed and moved it in front of her lips and left cheek, her eyes widening at the breath of cool air that grazed her skin like an invisible thread. Abd al-Reheem slept as Dalal ran her fair, plump fingers through his hair. A dark skinned nurse walked in and said cheerfully, "So Dalal, how's your husband doing?"

"He's good, Miss Salwa. Come have some oranges."

"No, thank you."

The nurse made for the oxygen tube and turned off the spigot. She put her hands in the pocket of her short white coat and pointed her head to Nargis. "Your mother?"

"No, she's my aunt, Abd al-Reheem's sister."

"Hello Auntie," and she turned and left. Nargis followed her firm bottom with her eyes and said, "Hello, missie."

With his eyes closed Abd al-Reheem said, "You've always been a lowly woman."

"Abd al-Reheem, what's going on?" asked Nargis.

"This bitch wants to inherit from me while I'm still alive."

"All day he's like this, Auntie," said Dalal.

He opened his eyes and said, "Move your feet away from the water, Nargis."

She looked down at her dangling feet and at the dry tiles and when she asked him "What water?" he said, "In the canal."

And she wondered to herself, "What canal? We're in the hospital, not in the country."

"How's mother, Nargis?" asked Abd al-Reheem.

"She's good."

"And the kids?"

"Oh, Brother, they're all fine, just look after yourself."

He said, "Oh, Nargis, if young Abdalla would only memorize the multiplication table, it'd be great."

"He's already memorized it," said Dalal.

"Oh, be quiet."

"I swear he's memorized it."

"I swear no one's ruined him but you."

"Me?!"

"Yes." His head grew heavy on her chest, and he died.

She tried to straighten him up and when she couldn't, she knew he'd died. As soon as she let out a scream, Nargis found herself between life and death. The patient on the next bed woke up and sat up looking at them with his pale face and hollow eyes.

Dalal tried to get a hold of herself under the weight of Abd al-Reheem's body which she encircled with her arms, screaming all the while, which made Abd al-Reheem get up from his death and say angrily, "Why are you screaming in my ear like that?"

Dalal went all mute and confused and couldn't see straight. Nurse Salwa came in and asked, "What's wrong, Dalal, why are you screaming?"

Abd al-Reheem straightened up at hearing the nurse's voice and said, "I don't know what's gotten into her."

The nurse leaned over Nargis and patted her on the cheek, "Get up, Auntie, the patient's fine." Nargis opened her eyes as she lay on the tiled floor. "How could you, Abd al-Reheem?" and she wiped her eyes with her small kerchief, smiling.

🐦

Muhammad Effendi al-Rashidi went up on the roof and looked down at his son's car parked in front of the building, and at Umm Hussein the grocer who was busy selling bread. He looked up at the rooftops strung with clotheslines and thought about how that idiot Umm Hussein had blocked the road with her wooden crates, so that for any car to go through on its way to the market she had to get up and drag the crates to the store's doorstep. He leaned over and saw Fadlallah Uthman from its beginning, and when he saw that it was empty with no cars coming, he felt annoyed and went to stand by the dusty cactus in one corner of the roof. He looked at the dry and cracked soil inside its round earthenware pot and thought to go to the bathroom and fill the large glass to water it.

He went down the stairs slowly without looking at his open apartment door and when he reached the ground floor, he stood outside the half-open door and knocked on its glass panel. "Come in, whoever is knocking." Muhammad Effendi quietly pushed open the wooden door and heard its slow creaking. He stood still letting his eyes get used to the darkness and saw Abdalla's mother, Nargis, sitting in the corner of the living room. He went in and sat on the edge of the sofa, gathering his gallabiya in his lap. "Good morning, Umm Abduh."

"Hello, Mr. Muhammad, welcome." With her small eyes she looked at his metal watch chain attached to a buttonhole and dangling on his chest, and told him none of the kids were home to make him a cup of tea.

"No need. I just have something to say and then I'll leave."

He looked up at the framed picture of al-Bahey Uthman hanging on the wall painted a faded green, then looked down at his feet clad in his wife's slippers, and thought that it was an enlarged version of the same picture the deceased had taken at the photography studio by the river. He asked her if she knew that they had bought a Model Fiat 128 car and Nargis said, "Of course. It's been months now." She added that she'd seen his wife Umm Hanan back then in the courtyard feeding the chickens and congratulated her. "The day right after you bought the car," she said.

Muhammad Effendi said he'd heard, then added, "But I was very upset when I saw your son deflating the tire."

"My son?"

"Every day, I swear."

"Which one? Abdalla, Samir, or Salama?"

"I don't know, one of them."

Nargis said, "But how, when the government has Abdalla, and Samir and Salama hardly come around, and each of the girls is living with her husband and kids?"

"But they visit you."

"Even so. They're grown men now, Abu Hanan."

He said, "Abdalla, Samir, and Salama are like my own kids, and if it was all just a matter of once or twice, I wouldn't have minded, let them play as they wish." He made clear to her that it was okay since it was a Model 128 and its engine was horizontal. "That's how the 128 is." Its engine was horizontal, and it was his private car, "But I intend to use it as a taxi," he said. "I have to get it registered as a cab which costs a lot of money and it could take a month or a year, God knows. And I think it's really shameful if they spent all this time deflating the tire, and I'd inflate it, and they'd empty it again and I'd inflate it again."

Nargis got up from the couch, saying, "This kind of talk won't do and is completely unacceptable." She scurried out of the living room and into the courtyard and lifted her kerchiefed head, calling out, "Umm Hanan! Hey you, Umm Hanan!"

Abu Hanan left while she was still calling. He descended the few steps and stood by the building entrance where the car was parked. He stayed this way until he heard a sound like a muffled whistle. He stepped forward and saw the little girl in her green satin gallabiya squatting by the rear tire holding a wooden matchstick. She stuffed it into the air valve and the air rushed out, and she closed her eyes as it blew her soft hair. He crossed the street slowly and stood in front of Umm Hussein the grocer. "Good morning, Umm Hussein."

She took a round loaf of bread from in front of her and flung it to the far edge of the wooden crate. "Hello," she replied.

"Your granddaughter, every day, I swear, is deflating my car tires."

"So hit her."

"No, Umm Hussein, one must speak to those in charge. And since Abu Hussein died, you're the one responsible for the shop."

"And if I'm the one responsible for the shop, you want me to drop everything and go run after a kid?"

"Then what's to be done, Umm Hussein?"

"I told you and you're not satisfied. When you see her doing it again, break her neck," then she called out, "Get up, girl! I don't know what you like about that piece of junk." The little girl got up and ran off, laughing out loud.

Abu Hanan said if it was only a day or two he would have let her play, but this has been going on for a while now, and Umm Abdalla knows about the matter as well. He glanced at the mosque on the other side of the street and asked her, "Is it time for the noon prayer yet?"

Umm Hussein said she hadn't heard the call to prayer.

He turned and went back into the building, slowly pushing open the door and listening to its lazy creaking. He saw Umm Abdalla sitting in her place and thought to ask her where they had enlarged the deceased Abu Abdalla's photo and how much it had cost with the frame, but instead he went up to the roof. His young grandchild had raised his gallabiya above his protruding stomach and was urinating on the cactus. "Oh, you little dog!" said Abu Hanan. The little boy ran off laughing, still urinating with the gallabiya up over his stomach. He watched him as he went down the stairs, then went back to the edge of the roof and looked once more down at Fadlallah Uthman, the parked car, and Umm Hussein with her crates. When he spotted the little girl coming from afar he stood back quickly and concealed himself well. He thought he would leave her to play while he went to the bathroom to fill the large glass with water then come back and sprinkle it on her with his fingers. He looked over at the dusty cactus, the urine scattered on the leaves, cutting through the dust to reveal its darker clean color. He thought she must be squatting now with her green gallabiya, sticking the matchstick into the tire and giggling as the air blew through her hair. He tiptoed forward until he was close to the roof's edge, then he leaned over suddenly. But Muhammad Effendi al-Rashidi couldn't see her at all.

Nargis couldn't believe what Muhammad Effendi al-Rashidi had said about her children and the tire. She couldn't help but think of the difference between him and his father, the late Ahmad al-Rashidi. She could see him now, passing by her door as he came and went, his pot belly lifting his gallabiya and making it short in the front and long in the back, calling out,

"Greetings, Umm Abdalla." He was a station supervisor before he retired and no one ever challenged his word. His only fault was that he didn't pray, which angered the people over at the mosque. They sent over Hagg Mahmoud the coal dealer to talk to him, they also talked to his son Muhammad and Bahey to try to convince him, and finally they talked to him in person. He would always say "God willing" and then never go.

He remained healthy, his full-throated voice reaching all the way to the end of Fadlallah Uthman until those hoodlums, whom no one identified, assaulted and abused him, poor man. It was the blessed month of Ramadan at sunset, and he sat breaking the fast with his children around the low round table. The whole building heard the voice crying out for help, "Ahmad al-Rashidi!" He got up from the table and rushed out, calling "I'm coming!" When he opened the apartment door, he was hit in the face with a steel object that hashed his chin and nose and broke several teeth. It took the wind out of him and he landed on his back in a pool of blood, poor man. Everyone in the building went out onto the landing, but there wasn't a soul in Fadlallah Uthman.

Nargis looked at her half-open apartment door and felt frightened. She thought about her children and how the house was so empty now. She had given birth to twelve boys and girls, losing half of them when they were little, and because those who passed away never left her heart, she confused them with the ones who lived. She noticed this when conversation turned to her children, so she would count them on her fingers to distinguish the absent ones from the ones who stayed: Ihsan, Salama, Samir, and so on. May you rest in peace, Bahey, she thought. She remembered the day she went to visit her mother, staying barely a half hour to drink tea and then she returned with her brother Abd al-Reheem to find that Bahey had passed away wearing his underwear and the cap from the Postal Service. God was merciful and had her visit her mother at that particular moment.

Nargis wondered, "If I hadn't gone to see my mother, would Bahey still have died sitting on the couch in his underwear? Or when he was talking to me? Or when he was dressed and sleeping?" She asked God for forgiveness and remembered that Bahey had asked her to bring Abd al-Reheem's saw with her and that Abd al-Reheem was carrying it when they arrived. "I wonder what you wanted the saw for?" she thought. When she realized that she didn't know, sorrow overtook her and she said, "I wish I'd asked you, Bahey." And she wept as she sat alone.

"Did you hear that Basima died, Abd al-Reheem?" asked Nargis. He looked at her with his exhausted eyes. The power was out in Fadlallah Uthman and the kerosene lamp on top of the television let out a faint red glow that the breeze turned into willowy shadows. "I swear, she died," she said.

"Who told you?"

"Zeinab, Ali Mansour's daughter."

"Was she sick?"

"She didn't say."

Abd al-Reheem straightened up a little from his seat on the couch, emaciated in his linen gallabiya, his right foot grazing his sister's knee as she sat on the rug spread out between the two couches. The blue teapot was on the lit burner, and the tea kit was on the china tray with the old metal border, next to the stalks of mint with their dry leaves.

"Umm Hanafi was a little under the weather. I went to see her and saw Zeinab there. You know her, don't you? Ali Mansour's daughter, the one who owned the old house."

"Yes, I know her. She's his youngest, right?"

"Young? You should see her now, she's a school principal!" said Nargis as she peered through the open apartment door to the building's dark courtyard, pricking up her ears and clamping her toothless mouth. The top of the teakettle began to rumble as the water boiled, and she busied herself with pouring the tea. Abd al-Reheem came to at the clinking of the spoon in the teacups.

"I felt sorry for her, that one. I kept crying the whole time I was there. Umm Hanafi and I took turns crying—we nearly went blind!" She dried her eyes with the edge of her black gallabiya and sighed, "Oh well, God forgive us all."

Abd al-Reheem understood what Nargis was getting at. And he thought to say as he had many years ago that she wasn't a tramp as was rumored. He thought to reveal to Nargis now, for the first time, that it was Basima who refused to marry him, that he was ready to do anything for her, even sell the land. Abd al-Reheem wanted to say this to Nargis but he thought to himself, "Forget it, boy. It won't do any good." The hissing of the burner stopped abruptly as Nargis turned it off and her facial features disappeared in the darkness. Abd al-Reheem lifted the cup of tea and inhaled the mint.

How long has it been now, twenty years, twenty-five, thirty? He used to furtively go up to her room on the rooftop. The wardrobe faced the door, the bed was on the right, and on the other side, underneath the large, open window (he could see the sky through it when he lay on the bed) she had a vanity with an oval mirror, small and shiny. On the vanity stand she had a tube of lipstick, lotion, a comb, a bottle of perfume, talcum powder, and kohl. She had two dresses, a light yellow one with red flowers and a belt, and a wool two-piece, and lots of satin underpants and revealing nightgowns. She put on makeup and lined her eyes, going up and down the stairs and chatting and joking with the neighbors all day. She had a beautiful ,fair body and smooth, round shoulders, and she never changed her ways even with all the tongue-wagging, so they called her "Basima a la Mode" and accused her of being a tramp.

He remembered when they were alone in her room once, he left first so they could catch a movie at Cinema Olympie near the Ataba Post Office where he worked. He was by the door, she by the open wardrobe, her thick head of styled hair tilted to one side. Her right hand rested on her waist and her left held the half open wardrobe door, contemplating her few, bright-colored clothes. He told her to hurry up but to no avail. First she looked at them all together, then she studied each one, straightening this one, touching that one, rearranging the folded items on the nearly empty shelves after she gave him her first husband's clothes. He left while she was still standing, happy with her clothes and undecided about what to wear. When she caught up with him later, wearing one of the two dresses, she looked like a bride, perfumed and radiant.

She used to laugh. Sometimes her finery embarrassed him, and sometimes her loud voice mortified him. He remembered her angry features and surprise. "Are you ashamed of me, Abd al-Reheem?" Then she cried. She cried the whole way, in front of passersby, and didn't care. She refused to forgive him or ride the tram, but in the morning they made up. She started to treat him like all the other residents, smiling and saying hello. But she never went out with him again.

Abd al-Reheem took a last sip of tea and reached out to her. She gazed in silence, and he smiled in the faint light, spotting the wet mint leaves on the loose tea grounds.

As she sat in her favorite place between the two couches, Nargis thought that the first thing she'd do when "God eased things a bit" would be to buy a china platter for the rice and a big serving bowl for the soup, in place of the ones she used to have long ago that broke. She thought about this and was amazed, because she had sold all her gold jewelry, her mother Hanem's filigreed necklace, and her grandmother Aziza's ankle bracelet. And her husband's dowry gift: the bracelets and the heavy door-knocker earrings. She sold all her copper cookery: the pots and the colander and the old pitcher, the big washing tub and the serving spoon. She sold it all during hard times, even her beautiful china set. Only the tea tray remained after one piece after the other was smashed: the large and small plates, the tea and coffee cups and their small decorated plates, the sugar and cream set and the small salt shaker. Nargis thought of all this and was amazed that she had no desire to make up for any of it. She thanked God she had them when things were tight and the money they brought kept their heads high among everyone. But she always hoped to have the oval china rice platter and the large soup tureen, with its tiny flowers and the cover with the round gold bauble on top.

Many things got lost as she sat in her favorite place between the two couches. Their memories came back to her, just as the memories of people long gone returned. Her high bed that ended up in pieces, its four high posters disassembled. It had ornamented black panels fringed with small copper balls that Abdalla used to unscrew when he was little and use as marbles to play with the other kids. The bed's posters, panels, and beechwood bed plate were piled up in the courtyard behind the stairs, and its place was occupied by a low wide bed with plain iron panels. Nargis didn't know why she had allowed this or how she could have left her old bed to get ruined by the summer heat and winter rain until it was destroyed and lost bit by bit. Only one out of four copper figurines was left. Each one had had an hourglass figure, with an embroidered waist and a small opening that latched onto the top of the bedpost. The edges of the light tulle canopy then tied onto the figurines.

The figurines would suddenly appear and then disappear. At first, one got lost, then the second, and third. Only the last one remained, disappearing every now and then. She found it in the stairwell, washed it and buffed it, then left it in a set place. But it would disappear again for a year or two, then she'd find it with one of the kids or trip over it or it would roll out when she was pulling something from under the bed. She'd put it away in a safe place and as the days went by, it vanished again. To keep it still, she hid it under the folded clothes or between the two mattresses or behind Abdalla's books before he moved out and took them. But as time passed, she forgot where she hid it.

Nargis got up. By the end of the day she was back sitting on the rug, her kerchief slipping from her white-streaked hair. Spread out around her were all the knick-knacks from under the bed and the couches, from the kitchen and the locked television cabinet and the wardrobe, the clothes in storage and the cap Bahey was looking for and wore the day he died. Everything was all over the floor and on the overturned cushions. Her toothless mouth was clamped shut and her fevered face had dried. She gazed at the figurine, turning it in her lap and wiping the dust from its old embroidered copper, thinking of a place where she could put it and never lose sight of it.

6

IT'S NIGHTTIME, AND the clinic is on the ground floor of a building without a door on Fadlallah Uthman. A big reception area with motley chairs, but the dust-colored parquet floor is well swept. Mr. Abdalla sits to the right of the small desk, the old male nurse stands by the curtain of the exam room, and over there, a faded picture of a woman feeding a baby from her bare breast. The light is faint and the paint is chipping off the walls.

Abdalla is waiting for the doctor. He tries over and over again to retrieve some of what's left in his memory, from when his mother used to bring him here as a boy. He remembers a young, smiling face, its features now lost to him. He remembers kinky or coarse hair, a reddish color. It must have changed now. He knew his mother had great confidence in the doctor, Fadlallah Uthman's old doctor and the nearest one to their house. Even though now her children and children's children go to the young doctor in the joint clinic above the mosque, never does the topic of illness come up without her mentioning Dr. Rifaat in some way. "Dr. Rifaat treated it and it was perfect." Or she'd say, "When Dr. Rifaat first opened, his fee was only five piasters." "Don't judge by this messy clinic he's in now. They say he has another one, a big one in Bab al-Louq, with a very expensive examination fee." "You won't believe this, Abdalla my son, yesterday when I was going to Grandmother Hanem I saw Dr. Rifaat coming out of the car. I didn't recognize him, diabetes has worn him down, poor man."

The curtain shook a little and the old doctor walked out followed by a young woman carrying a child and arranging his clothes. He sat behind the crowded desk and shuffled papers while Abdalla stared at the smiling, strange face. He heard him say, "What day is it today, Hagg Shawqi?"

"Thursday," said Hagg Shawqi in a thin voice as he packed the small, dark briefcase.

"I'll see him Monday," he said, extending the slip of paper to the woman without looking at her. "Give him a spoonful as soon as you get home, then one in the morning. Two spoonfuls every day." He fiddled with a glass full of spoons, selected one and held it out in front of the young woman. "This size."

"Yes, Doctor."

Abdalla noticed it was medium-sized, between a tablespoon and a small teaspoon. "You won't find a spoon this size, so give him a spoonful and a half of the spoons you've got, and feed him milk." As she walked out he added, "Don't forget to shake the bottle before you give him the medicine."

"God bless you, Doctor."

"Goodbye." He turned to Abdalla, smiling.

They went out to Fadlallah Uthman, walking by the light of the few light bulbs hanging over the closed storefronts. The male nurse walked ahead of them carrying the briefcase. When they reached the building's open entrance, Abdalla went in first. While the doctor was examining her, he leaned over his mother and whispered, "Dr. Rifaat, Ma."

He didn't receive an answer. Nargis had been in a coma for days. The doctor returned the blood pressure gauge to the nurse, who folded it carefully into the open briefcase on his knees. He made his way to the sofa and sat in the middle of the children and grandchildren who crowded the place. "How long has she been like this?"

The young girl, Nargis, spoke up, her eyes red from crying, "Today is the fourth day." The doctor shook his head as he sat underneath Bahey's photo hanging on the wall.

While they were moving her upper body to arrange her clothes, Nargis woke from her coma and the kerchief slipped off her heavy head, revealing her coal-and-silver hair. "Is any part of me uncovered, kids?" she asked.

"No, Ma." Young Nargis leaned over and pulled down the gallabiya to her grandmother's feet.

"Abdalla, take care of your brothers and sisters."

"Don't say such things, Ma!" cried out the girls.

They cried, patting her shoulder and kissing her bare head as they rested her back on the sofa's backrest on top of which were arranged the many boxes of medicine. As she leaned back, she reached her hand out as if holding onto something. Her eldest daughter Ihsan reached out for her hand, and Nargis held it to her mouth and kissed it.

"Don't. If you really love her, you should pray for her," said the doctor.

Back on Fadlallah Uthman, he said, "God willing, she'll improve, because we need to run a few tests on her at the hospital. Right now, poor thing, she can't go anywhere."

"She seems very sick to me, Doctor," said Abdalla.

The doctor moved his head and watched the nurse walk ahead of them. "Yes, she's sick." He rubbed the front of his shoe on Fadlallah Uthman's pavement and said, "She can sit up, talk, laugh. But go back to what she was like before? That's difficult."

Without losing his sad smile, he looked up, his face illuminated by the light bulb over Hagg Mahmoud the coal dealer's store, his short hair white, save for a few reddish bits. As he resumed staring, it seemed to Abdalla that some of the features of the young doctor suddenly appeared but just as soon gave way to this tired, old face, as if it was him, but not him. He moved off down the dark road.

$\clubsuit$

Fadlallah Uthman was silent and completely abandoned save for them and the long wooden streetlights naked of bulbs, the plaited clotheslines, the heavy, folded textiles of the large outdoor pavilions, the palm crates full of light bulbs and twisted electrical cords, and the hole-filled plastic plates. Mr. Abdalla took a step back and looked through the open living room window to the glass panel on the door of the dark inner room where she was spending her last night. He knew she was afraid of the dark and asked, "Is there a light bulb in that room?"

"It went out a long time ago," said his younger brother, and added that it was just laziness that kept them from replacing it, and also, their mother never used to go into that room.

A few days ago when they moved her from her place between the couches to the inner room for the sake of her visitors, his sister Hanem told him that their mother hadn't stepped into that room since his father had died. Abdalla was taken aback because he'd spent years with them after his father's death and had never noticed that. As he came and went, he saw her sitting or sleeping in her corner in front of the television or with her elbow on the cushion and her chin in her palm looking out the window. He would sit with her a bit and then leave, thinking that she stayed there just during her siesta or late at night.

"Oh Ma, . . . Ma. Didn't the doctor say not to eat any salty foods?" he would say.

"Come on, Abdalla, son, what if one suddenly drops dead? Do you want them to die without having what they really want?"

And so you pass away, bereft of everything you ever wanted, except salty foods.

"The table lamp has a bulb," said Salama. Abdalla crossed Fadlallah Uthman, climbed the few steps and went through the apartment's open door. The mothers were leaning their heads on the wall, and the children were sleeping under the covers on the two couches. He removed the light bulb from the table lamp and made for the inner room. He opened the door, and the living room light rested on the edge of the bed. Grandmother Hanem was sitting behind his mother, who was covered with the printed green tablecloth his wife had given her for Mother's Day. Hanem was whispering to her daughter and didn't notice him come in. He pulled up a chair and stood on it to replace the bulb, but when he turned on the light it didn't work. He returned the chair and left the door slightly ajar to let the living room light seep in.

Ihsan stayed awake until they came back from the burial grounds. The girls had prepared the living room to receive the women giving their condolences. She asked Dalal to take the kids to her house and Hanan to take care of making the coffee, and she seated herself next to her grandmother, welcoming the neighboring women and her departed mother's dear ones. The sun hadn't started seeping into the window when they gathered in their black clothes and sat all around the room leaning on the walls and spilled out onto the steps leading to Fadlallah Uthman. They left the space under the window for the cross-legged, female Qur'an reciter with the manly voice and the black sunglasses that slipped to reveal the white of her one open eye. In front of her, a woman's clean slipper was jammed under the heavy, round base that held up the short stand, making the amplifier lean toward her. There was also a clean glass ashtray and a china tray printed with a green bough surrounded by small red roses.

The eldest daughter surveyed the faces that appeared suddenly, the faces that she knew from the neighborhood and those she didn't recognize. She wished her mother Nargis was there to see what time had done to so-and-so's mother and so-and-so's aunt, and she felt dizzy inhaling the scent of storage from the clothes that had been pulled out of the depths of wardrobes. She looked over at her tiny grandmother, Hanem, who had withdrawn into her veil, only the tip of her delicate nose and light moustache visible. Hanem took a while to respond to someone giving her their condolences, would miss their hand outstretched in greeting, or all of a sudden laugh and look down trying to hide her giggles. Yet when she did speak her voice was audible and clear.

Umm Hanan's weeping grew louder as she whispered into her veil, "Oh my dear Nargis, Umm Abdalla." Ihsan let the tears roll freely down her ruddy cheeks. Just then, the young Nargis left her bed and came out of the inner room, standing there half-sleeping and taken by the black, sobbing circle. Like a large fruit that was just ripening, she craned her neck, her soft breast spilled out of the torn strap of her nightgown, and she unfolded to reveal the thick shadow where her thighs met. Her swelling form took shape, and her lap was tinged with a new spot of blood.

Ihsan gazed at her daughter as she prepared to get up, whispering, "Nargis, girl." But the girl turned in a peculiar fashion, receiving the rays of the sun that were now pouring through the living room window. A halo of fire and frizz formed around her disheveled hair, and her full lips parted. She moved away.

They'd finished having tea and were chatting a lot, remembering and smiling. "May you rest in peace, Ma," said Ihsan with her sad face and eyes cleansed from all the crying. Her head was tied with the black kerchief and she sat holding the teacup by the television stand, which they'd covered with a big faded towel. They heard a soft rapping on the door's glass panel. It was Umm Rizq, who came and went all day in her black wrap and thin, skinny frame. She looked into the living room from her place by the door and said, "Greetings, everyone."

"Hello."

"May you live long and remember."

"May you live a long life," they replied.

She gathered the ends of the black wrap around her face and whispered, "Can I have a word, Umm Nargis?" and went down the few steps leading to the street and waited. Ihsan followed her. Umm Rizq said she wanted something of the deceased's effects.

"Sure, what would you like?" asked Ihsan.

"The red velvet shawl."

"Red velvet shawl?"

"It'll keep me warm and remind me of her." Ihsan was taken aback and said that her mother, may she rest in peace, had no red shawl, but Umm Rizq insisted. Ihsan swore that her mother had never in her whole life worn anything red.

"Then who used to wear a red velvet shawl?"

"Here in our building?"

"I think so."

"I really don't know."

"Maybe it's Umm Khalil who lives up the street?"

"Maybe."

She narrowed her eyes and said, "It's got to be Umm Khalil, there's no one else."

Ihsan asked her if she'd like something else of her mother's, a gallabiya maybe? Umm Rizq was astonished, "Oh my God! A gallabiya?" She gathered up her wrap and said, "What kind of talk is that, Umm Nargis?" She turned angrily and left.

"I'm going to check in on your grandmother and come right back," said Abd al-Reheem. Abdalla looked at his uncle's face, which collapsed without his dentures, and said, "You want me to come with you, Uncle?"

"No, you stay with your sisters."

He walked to the end of Fadlallah Uthman and opened the door, crossed the big room and made his way to the covered courtyard. He stopped by the water storage urn and peered through the small open door into the room. The grandmother sat on the old rug in her black gallabiya, her small head facing the large, engraved chest at an angle. "Greetings, Ma," he said.

"Who is it?" she said without blinking.

"It's me, Abduh."

"Come in, dear."

He stood silently, leaning his big head into the room. "How's your sister Nargis doing, Abduh?" she asked.

"Nothing, Ma."

"I said your sister Nargis, boy."

"She's fine."

"Did the doctor see her?"

"Yes."

"So is she up yet or what?"

"Not yet."

"Are her kids there?"

"Yes."

"Did Abdalla return home?"

"All of them are there, Ma."

"You left them alone to come here?"

"I'm going right back."

"Do you see my slippers anywhere?"

"Why?"

"Get me the slippers boy, let me go see her."

"Tomorrow morning I'll take you."

"Did you see Abd al-Rahman?"

"I'll travel to see him on the first of the month."

"Did you talk to him about the plot of land?"

"I did."

"How'd you talk to him, boy, if you haven't traveled yet?"

"I talked to him before and I'll speak to him about it again."

"Take Abdalla with you."

He straightened up. "Do you need anything?"

"Make sure to come back before night falls, boy. And say hello to your father, Abdel Qader, and your uncle, Abd al-Aziz. Goodbye."

He returned to the big room, turned on the naked bulb hanging from the high ceiling, and sat on the couch, looking around at the faded wall paint, his framed photo from when he was a young man in his Postal Service suit, and the Asyut-style chairs with their wooden armrests pointing toward the high bed. His eyes rested on the torn sheet; he gathered it under him and rested his elbow on the couch armrest beneath the big, shuttered window.

The tune came to him from the depths of the house: *The*

caller called out and I heard him with my own ears, he who loses his brother can never make up for him.

He rested his head on his palm and turned on his side, the tears flowing quietly, then his jaw began to tremble. He sobbed without a sound, as if chewing the weeping inside his toothless mouth.

On the way to the hospital, Salama said Umm Hanan had gone ahead to Sidi Omar to oversee the opening of the burial grounds and that Abu Khaled hadn't gone to work so he could wash the body. Mr. Abdalla asked, "Who's Abu Khaled?"

"Our brother-in-law."

"Does he know how to perform the washing?"

"Quite probably."

"And what if he doesn't know?"

"Hagg Mahmoud is with him."

"Who's Hagg Mahmoud?"

"The coal dealer."

"Does he know?"

"He must. It's not a big deal, and besides, our cousins are worthier of the money than giving it to a ritual washer man we don't know."

When they reached the hospital, Dalal spotted them and started wailing with a number of women from Fadlallah Uthman. Mr. Abdalla joined the men, and after a while, a voice from the small ward called out, "Mr. Abdalla." He looked round him and the voice said, "Come in."

"You're the eldest," said Salama, with a clear look of reproach in his eyes.

"What do you mean?"

"You have to attend the washing." An old woman with a kerchief tied around her head came up to him and gave him a light package. "Take this with you, dear, when you go in,"she said. He took it from her and walked off.

Hagg Mahmoud the coal dealer stuck his face out from the open door and pulled him in, smiling, "How are you, Abdalla, son?" Then he frowned, "May he rest in peace." He wore his traditional dark gallabiya, his wool skullcap pushed back on his head. Abdalla's brother-in-law had his sleeves and gallabiya hem rolled up and stood behind a high basin made of cement overlaid with white tile. His uncle, Abd al-Reheem, lay in the basin, his nose plugged and pointing upward. Abdalla stood around confused until his brother-in-law reached out and took the packet from him, unwrapping it. It contained a yellow loofa, a scented bar of soap with a picture of a pretty woman on the wrapping, and a bottle of cologne.

"Is the loofa soft?" said Mahmoud with his husky voice.

"Perfect," said Abu Khaled.

"Let me see," he rubbed it in his palm with the coal blackened fingernails. He turned to Abdalla and said, "If it's rough it could hurt him. See, as long as we're alive we can withstand pain but as soon as we die, our skin becomes thin and anything can affect it." He returned the loofa to Abu Khaled who said, "Give me a hand." They raised up Abd al-Reheem so that he was in a sitting position. Abdalla supported his back, Abu Khaled pulled the gallabiya from under him while Hagg Mahmoud lifted first one arm and then the other, taking off his cotton undershirt. When his upper body was completely naked they returned him to the prone position. Abdalla moved back a bit under the weight of the corpse, pulling his hands out before his uncle's head could rest in the basin, and his rear end bumped lightly but firmly on the cement. Abu Khaled cast him a quick reproachful glance, and Abdalla shuddered and thought to himself, "Sorry, Uncle." And he noticed that his uncle gave him a heedless smile.

Abu Khaled pulled off Abd al-Reheem's cotton underpants and turned on a tap with a long, transparent plastic hose attached to it, letting the water run over Abd al-Reheem's head, then started rubbing him with the soap. Abdalla gazed at the soap and water running over his uncle's face; his half-closed eyes didn't blink. While Abu Khaled was turning him on his side Abd al-Reheem's hand moved to cover his private parts. "Good God!" cried out the Hagg.

"There is no God but God," said Abdalla in a choked voice. Suddenly, Hagg Mahmoud said, "Wait, Abu Khaled." Abu Khaled's hand was suspended in midair as the water poured from the hose onto Abd al-Reheem's mouth and nose. The Hagg looked at both of them and said, "We're forgetting something very important." He was silent for a second, then added, "Anyone who's not pure has to leave." He looked at Abdalla, "No offense, folks, we're in the presence of angels." Then he straightened, "Go ahead."

Abu Khaled was soaping the chest, stomach, and arms, and when Abd al-Reheem's hands slipped and his genitals were exposed, the Hagg said, "Leave him be." Abu Khaled covered them with a small white towel and cleaned underneath it, then cleaned the legs and the toes, one by one. He moved back and contemplated the whole body, "How's that?"

"Not yet," smiled the Hagg.

"Why?"

"The purification."

"Not only that, the ablutions too," said Abu Khaled. His smile widened, "Don't worry, I know what I'm doing."

"Truth be told, you're doing great so far."

Abu Khaled started spraying Abd al-Reheem with the water,

half-covering the opening of the hose with his thumb, repeating in singsong, "There is no god but God, in the name of God."

"Testify to the oneness of God!" cried out Hagg Mahmoud.

"There is no god but God," Mr. Abdalla replied.

Abu Khaled finished reciting the Qur'anic chapter "Say he is God the One," and the Hagg wrapped gauze round the lower jaws and the head, and Abd al-Reheem looked to his nephew to be suffering from tonsilitis. They brought over the burial shroud, rolled up like a light carpet, and turned Abd al-Reheem on his side. Abdalla supported his back with both hands until they wrapped it, then turned him over onto his other side and pulled the end of the shroud over him and removed the small towel covering his genitals. Abdalla moved back to make room for them. The shroud was about a foot too long at the head and feet. His brother-in-law tied and folded the extra cloth and Hagg Mahmoud stepped up and tied it around his uncle's body with a clean piece of cloth around the waist like a belt. He opened the bottle of cologne and sprayed its contents over Abd al-Reheem in his snug swaddle until the place was filled with the scent of soap and lemon cologne.

"Bring over the panel of wood," said the Hagg, and he opened the door. Abdalla ibn Uthman found himself calling out in the open air, "Bring over the panel of wood," and his voice echoed, "Bring over the panel of wood."

The sun was shining and it was hot. He sat leaning his back against the wall of the small ward. He saw them crowding around the bier on their way to the long dark car. They put in the casket and closed the car's rear door. He heard brief feminine whining, and then everyone hurried in all different directions.

7

DALAL WOKE UP, took a clean metal bowl and the small boy Abdalla by the hand, and called out in the direction of the far room, "Good morning, Ma."

"Are you up, Dalal?" came the reply from the courtyard roof. Dalal looked for the old woman but couldn't see her in the darkness; she replied, "Yes, I'm up."

"Did the kids go to school?"

"Today's Friday, there's no school."

"Fine, come in, dear."

"I'm going out."

"You're going out, Dalal?"

"Just to the shop. Abdalla's hungry." And the boy cried out, "Hanem!"

"Did he say, 'Hanem'?"

"Yes, the little brat."

"Hee, hee, hee—d'you know me, boy?"

"Sure, Ma, he's not a baby." She made for the door, and the old woman said, "Did you go out, Dalal?"

"I'm just about to."

"Don't be late, Abd al-Reheem is on his way." Dalal turned and opened the door. She went out onto Fadlallah Uthman and passed by her aunt Nargis's dusty shuttered window. Abdalla raised his head and said, "Auntie Nargis is dead." She pulled his hand, and he said, "And Abd al-Reheem is dead, and Hanem doesn't know."

"Be quiet, boy."

"But she doesn't understand a thing."

"Listen, Abdalla boy, don't you dare talk to her about these things."

"Aren't Abd al-Reheem and my Auntie Nargis her kids?"

"Yes, they're her kids."

"Fine, then it's none of my business."

She bought the fuul and on the way back she said to him, "Abd al-Reheem, he's your father."

"Yes, I know."

"Then how can you say it's none of your business?"

"Isn't he the one who went to the hospital and died?"

"God has his ways."

"Is everything God's ways?"

Dalal pushed open the door and stepped down into the shade and humidity. The old woman's voice called out again, "Don't close the door, Abd al-Reheem, Dalal's out."

"Yes, Ma."

"Dalal, you're here."

"I'm here."

"Is Abd al-Reheem with you?"

Dalal busied herself with sprinkling some salt and drizzling oil over the fuul, and she took a round loaf of bread from the hanging sack.

"Dalal, can you hear me?"

"Yes, I hear you," replied Dalal in a choked voice. The old woman's face frightened her as it floated past, radiant with greenery, in the darkness behind the water urn, and then disappeared.

The grandmother reached out for her old slippers. She put them on and walked down the long corridor below ground level. She stopped at the open door and climbed up. The light of day took her by surprise, and she started. She covered her mouth with her sheer black veil and stepped out onto Fadlallah Uthman, walking in the direction of Nargis's nearby house on the left. She touched the folded paper in her inside pocket, and thought to buy something so she didn't go empty handed. The clamor of a donkey-drawn cart blocked her way, and she stuck close to the wall, frightened. She turned with the donkey until the cart moved off and there was no danger, and she continued walking, but in the opposite direction, without knowing why.

"What's going on, uncle?"

Abd al-Reheem opened his eyes with difficulty from his slumber and said, "I'm fine." He smiled, "I'm not going to die before I take the land."

"Just get better."

His smile faded.

"Remember long ago, Uncle, when your fishing rod caught the sparrow?"

"Sparrow?" he said and surprise covered his face. "Did your mother tell you that Basima a la Mode is dead?"

"Yes."

He closed his eyes.

How did she know

To let her laughter peal out like that in the utter silence?

To choose a time when grief settled in one or two of the house's rooms and then let it out, brash, spurning misfortune, and filling the world with excitement and joy?

How did she know, she alone in her far, high room,
with the empty rooftops,
the night stars,
and the Nile?

He sat for a long while atop the sloping riverbank, white stubble on his chin. A young girl squatted by the water's edge, emptying her bladder underneath her stretched cotton gallabiya.

Abdalla ibn Uthman sits alone, looking out at Fadlallah Uthman, at the front of the dark courtyard situated several degrees below ground level where his grandmother and uncle used to spend their long nights. Looking up from the level of the doorjamb, the upper floors of the surrounding buildings disappear into the sky. With the slanted setting of the sun, the ends of the far houses become clear, and the place opens onto a piece of the night sky. A clear-blue, crooked curtain of stars falls. From here, Fadlallah Uthman is a billowy space of shadow and light. The lamps are red halos hanging over the few closed shops. Mr. Abdalla can't see what is at the center of each halo, but at its edges, when the light fades and the darkness turns diaphanous, he can sometimes make out a window shutter, or a door, or a trace of a wall.

Grandmother Hanem is still walking, looking for her daughter Nargis's house on the left, with its green-shuttered open window. She turns with the alleyways and wanders in the lanes, searching in people's faces, going in and out of houses and shops, looking, touching the glass storefronts with her delicate dry fingers, and giggling to herself. She hides her oddly greened face with her sheer black veil.

When night comes upon her, she takes refuge by the water, sitting her small frame underneath the low-growing castor-oil palms with their fan leaves drooping over the edge of the still river. She dozes off and awakens at the trembling of the silver dawn across the gloomy steel bridge. She wets her face, chews a handful of moist greens, and sits with her legs drawn up underneath her. She climbs up the sloping bank and stands there under the big, high camphor tree.

Grandmother Hanem dusts the hay off her dress and pricks up her ears at the approaching caravan of horse drawn carts coming from the direction of Qanater, carrying fresh produce. She follows the horses' trots as they're steered by sleeping men in the morning fog, listening to the tolling of the thin, swinging bells, following them as they trail off in the distance and die out one by one at the bend of the river. And she calls out, that someone may hear her, "Going out to the village, son?"

Modern Arabic Writing
from the American University in Cairo Press

Ibrahim Abdel Meguid *The Other Place* • *No One Sleeps in Alexandria*
Yahya Taher Abdullah *The Mountain of Green Tea*
Leila Abouzeid *The Last Chapter*
Ibrahim Aslan *Nile Sparrows*
Hala El Badry *A Certain Woman*
Salwa Bakr *The Wiles of Men*
Hoda Barakat *The Tiller of Waters*
Mourid Barghouti *I Saw Ramallah*
Mohamed El-Bisatie *A Last Glass of Tea* • *Houses Behind the Trees*
Clamor of the Lake
Fathy Ghanem *The Man Who Lost His Shadow*
Randa Ghazy *Dreaming of Palestine*
Tawfiq al-Hakim *The Prison of Life*
Yahya Hakki *The Lamp of Umm Hashim*
Bensalem Himmich *The Polymath*
Taha Hussein *A Man of Letters* • *The Sufferers* • *The Days*
Sonallah Ibrahim *Cairo: From Edge to Edge* • *Zaat* • *The Committee*
Yusuf Idris *City of Love and Ashes*
Denys Johnson-Davies *Under the Naked Sky: Short Stories from the Arab World*
Said al-Kafrawi *The Hill of Gypsies*
Edwar al-Kharrat *Rama and the Dragon*
Naguib Mahfouz *Adrift on the Nile* • *Akhenaten, Dweller in Truth*
Arabian Nights and Days • *Autumn Quail* • *The Beggar*
The Beginning and the End • *The Cairo Trilogy: Palace Walk*
Palace of Desire • *Sugar Street* • *Children of the Alley*
The Day the Leader Was Killed • *Echoes of an Autobiography*
The Harafish • *The Journey of Ibn Fattouma* • *Khufu's Wisdom*
Midaq Alley • *Miramar* • *Naguib Mahfouz at Sidi Gaber*
Respected Sir • *Rhadopis of Nubia* • *The Search* • *Thebes at War*
The Thief and the Dogs • *The Time and the Place*
Wedding Song • *Voices from the Other World*
Ahlam Mosteghanemi *Memory in the Flesh* • *Chaos of the Senses*
Buthaina Al Nasiri *Final Night*
Abd al-Hakim Qasim *Rites of Assent*
Somaya Ramadan *Leaves of Narcissus*
Lenin El-Ramly *In Plain Arabic*
Rafik Schami *Damascus Nights*
Miral al-Tahawy *The Tent* • *Blue Aubergine*
Bahaa Taher *Love in Exile*
Fuad al-Takarli *The Long Way Back*
Latifa al-Zayyat *The Open Door*